||| ||||| ||||||||||||||||||||||||||||||||
W9-ATN-638

Prescription: Romance™

"Are you? Desperate?"

Sarah laughed again and got up, pacing to the window. "No, of course not," she said, a little too quickly. "I'm quite happy like this, alone."

"Are you?" Matt was still sitting down, but she was terribly aware of him. "Aren't you ever tempted to have an affair?"

She turned slowly, wondering if she'd misunderstood him all along. "Is that a proposition?"

Caroline Anderson's nursing career was brought to an abrupt halt by a back injury, but her interest in medical things led her to work first as a medical secretary, and then, after completing her teacher training, as a lecturer in medical office practice to trainee medical secretaries. She lives in rural Suffolk, with her husband, two daughters, mother and assorted animals.

Prescription: Romance™

SARAH'S GIFT
CAROLINE ANDERSON

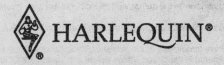

TORONTO • NEW YORK • LONDON
AMSTERDAM • PARIS • SYDNEY • HAMBURG
STOCKHOLM • ATHENS • TOKYO • MILAN • MADRID
PRAGUE • WARSAW • BUDAPEST • AUCKLAND

If you purchased this book without a cover you should be aware
that this book is stolen property. It was reported as "unsold and
destroyed" to the publisher, and neither the author nor the
publisher has received any payment for this "stripped book."

ISBN 0-373-63117-0

SARAH'S GIFT

First North American Publication 1999.

Copyright © 1999 by Caroline Anderson.

All rights reserved. Except for use in any review, the reproduction or
utilization of this work in whole or in part in any form by any electronic,
mechanical or other means, now known or hereafter invented, including
xerography, photocopying and recording, or in any information storage
or retrieval system, is forbidden without the written permission of the
publisher, Harlequin Enterprises Limited, 225 Duncan Mill Road,
Don Mills, Ontario, Canada M3B 3K9.

All characters in this book have no existence outside the imagination of
the author and have no relation whatsoever to anyone bearing the same
name or names. They are not even distantly inspired by any individual
known or unknown to the author, and all incidents are pure invention.

This edition published by arrangement with Harlequin Books S.A.

® and TM are trademarks of the publisher. Trademarks indicated with
® are registered in the United States Patent and Trademark Office, the
Canadian Trade Marks Office and in other countries.

Visit us at www.romance.net

Printed in U.S.A.

CHAPTER ONE

IT HAD been years since Sarah had noticed a man—five and a half, to be exact, and most of them not worth remembering.

She noticed this man, though.

Not that it was surprising. She would have had to be blind, deaf or hermaphrodite not to sit up and pay attention when he strolled through the double doors into the business end of Audley Memorial's A and E unit, one hand shoved casually into the pocket of his well-cut trousers, the other dangling a jacket over his shoulder on one finger.

Tall and fair, his rangy body wasn't lean enough to be lanky. It looked powerful, well put-together, with a look of Paul Newman about the grey eyes and a mouth just made for kissing. And laughing. And whispering sweet nothings. He also had no business just wandering onto the unit unannounced.

She slapped the file shut and stood up. 'Can I help you?'

His eyes dropped to her name badge, seeming to make a point of reading her name, then they flicked up and locked with hers, and a smile brushed his lips, just briefly. 'Sister Cooper—I'm Matt Jordan. I believe you're expecting me?'

His voice was deep, a little gravelly, with a soft Canadian accent that did odd things to the hairs on the back of her neck. How strange. She gave him a professional smile and ignored the shivers down her spine. 'Oh, yes. You've come to study us, like bugs under a microscope. Welcome to the Audley, Dr Jordan—and to England.' She went round the desk, held out her hand and had it swamped by long, strong fingers that wrapped around the back of her hand and engulfed it.

His touch was cool, dry, firm—and businesslike, so why did she experience that strange reaction? She had to fight the urge to snatch her hand back, but the next second, almost as if he knew she was uncomfortable, he freed her and smiled, sliding his hand easily back into that trouser pocket.

'I was told to report to the ER—sorry, A and E! Ryan O'Connor's expecting me.'

'Yes, he is, but he's tied up now, so you'll have to put up with me.'

He grinned. 'More likely to be the other way round, and I hope to learn from you, not treat you like a bug.'

She laughed. 'Whatever. I'm sure blood's red both sides of the pond. I'll have to write you out a glossary of abbreviations—in fact we'll get Ryan to do it as he's Canadian too.'

'At least we both speak the same language.' Laughter touched his mouth, putting her at her ease instantly.

'I shouldn't bet on it, we've trained him pretty well,' she said with a chuckle. 'He's about somewhere—we're quiet this morning, by a miracle, although that will all change now I've gone and opened my big mouth. He's just seeing a couple of yesterday's patients who've come back for a check-up. He'll be along in a minute.'

His brows pleated together. 'How come you're quiet? What a luxury.'

Sarah laughed. 'Tell me about it. It won't last. With the cold snap we had over the weekend we've had a string of casualties. They had to call Jack Lawrence in overnight, and he's taken today off as a result so I expect the day will go to hell very shortly. It's unfortunate, really, because if he'd been here you might have stood a chance of a gentle introduction. As it is I expect you'll get dragged into Resus before long and flung in at the deep end. It's been a bit like that recently.'

He nodded knowingly. 'We have the same every year but usually a little earlier—our winters tend to be longer. Lots of tumbles?' he suggested.

She agreed. 'Lots. Mostly elderly people with fractured wrists and hips, some youngsters with wrists again or collar bones—the odd coccyx from landing on their bottoms. Then, of course, there are the RTAs—'

'Road Traffic Accidents?'

She nodded and smiled. 'That's right. You call them MVAs, I believe—Motor Vehicle Accidents?'

He nodded affirmatively and grinned again. 'Maybe we won't have such a communication problem.'

'I'm sure we'll cope. Most of the time we'll know what we're doing anyway, so it's automatic.' She cocked her head slightly on one side. 'Fancy a cup of tea or coffee? You've arrived at just the right time. All my delegating's done and my paperwork's up to date, so I can sit back and relax for five minutes, knowing the only person I'm holding up is myself, and I reckon I deserve it after the weekend.'

His smile warmed the blue-grey depths of his rather gorgeous eyes. 'I'd love a cup of coffee. Breakfast seems a long time ago. I had to take my daughter to school on the way here, and the traffic was a bit heavy by the time I finished getting lost.'

She chuckled. 'The traffic round here's always a bit heavy. We get used to it. Come on, let's go and check the coffee machine. Patrick might have put it on, otherwise it'll be instant or wait for the machine to finish.'

'We'll go for instant,' he said without hesitation. 'If we wait someone'll try and waste themselves and we won't get it at all.' He followed her down the corridor, his firm, light tread keeping pace with her businesslike bustle easily. 'Do you get many MVAs—sorry, RTAs?'

'Enough. We're well sited for picking up the nasties that happen on the through trunk routes. Although it's a rural area we're bisected by busy roads with heavy commuter traffic and lots of freight movements, and so we get accidents, particularly if the weather closes in suddenly like it did on Saturday.'

She led him into the staffroom and found that it shrank to half its size. Matt Jordan seemed to fill it, propped against the worktop with his arms folded and a lazy grin on his face, watching her as she switched on the kettle and then picked up two mugs. 'Instant OK? Patrick's failed us.'

He nodded. 'I'll get used to it.'

Sarah snorted. 'Or learn to like tea.' She filled the coffee-machine and flicked the switch to turn it on. 'Did your daughter settle into school all right?'

He frowned and scrubbed a hand round the back of his neck. 'I hope so. I didn't have time to stop and worry, but she went in with Ryan O'Connor's children, so I think she'll be OK. The O'Connors have been great, really helpful.'

'Did you know him before? Is that why you chose the Audley for your research?'

Matt shook his head. 'It's just coincidence that he's a fellow Canadian, but it made a link. He's been really helpful, especially with Em. I hope she's OK.'

'Ring the school—ask.'

'And do what if they say she's unhappy? I'm at work—and, anyway, she'll cope. She's used to fitting in. She's moved around a lot in her short life.'

Sarah poured the hot water into the mugs and stirred. 'Can't your wife go if there's a problem?'

'I don't have a wife,' he said, in a voice that brooked no further discussion. Sarah took the hint. There were things she didn't talk about, too, things you didn't want to get out and air. She could respect that. She moved on.

'So how are you dealing with the after-school and weekends and being on call?' she asked, concerned to make sure he'd covered all his bases. 'Have you managed to sort all that sort of thing out already?'

'I have a neighbour—or rather Ryan does—who will fetch her from school and sit with her until I get to pick her up. When I'm on call overnight Ryan said she can go to them until I sort out a better arrangement.'

Sarah nodded. Arranging for child care was difficult, especially if you were new to an area. She'd had to do it once...

'There's a crèche in the hospital, did you know?' she suggested.

His smile was crooked and rather enchanting. 'I think my five-year-old daughter might draw the line at going in a crèche, somehow.'

Five. Sarah felt a pang, and suppressed it. There were lots of five-year-old girls. Literally hundreds of thousands—probably millions the world over. And nine- and seven-year-old boys.

She slopped milk into one mug and cocked a brow at him, putting the thoughts away. 'White?'

He shook his head. 'Black, please, no sugar. That's fine. Cheers.'

His fingers brushed hers and yet again there was that strange reaction, that little shimmy of the pulse that came out of nowhere.

'So, how long have you been here?' he asked, settling himself in one of the easy chairs with his outstretched legs shrinking the room again. She stirred her coffee and tried to forget about his blatant masculinity.

'Two years. I started as a staff nurse—I became Junior Sister just over a year ago.'

'And do you like it?'

'The hospital or the work?'

'Either.'

She smiled. 'I like both. They're a very friendly bunch here. The doctors are all very civilised and approachable, and the nursing staff make a well-knit team. It's a good place to work, if you can cope with the gallows humour.'

He laughed. 'I don't know a single trauma unit where the staff don't have a really sick line in patter. It goes with the territory—it's just a way of defusing the distress. If you didn't do it, you'd burn out in no time.'

Her smile was wry. 'People don't understand, though, unless they work there too. They think we're saints, but if they heard some of the things that were said we'd fall off our pedestals big time.'

'It helps if you have a partner who understands,' he said, and she wondered if his wife hadn't understood and if that had been the problem. He didn't give her time to dwell, though, just carried on. 'Didn't Ryan's wife work here?'

'Yes, and Jack Lawrence's, and Patrick's.'

'A regular dating agency.'

She laughed. 'Sounds like it, doesn't it? I think it's just the pressure. There's not much time to meet anyone else, and if you're working together intensively you get very close. You have to learn to trust people and rely on them, and it's only a short step from there to commitment. I won't say romance, there's precious little of that around here.'

He snorted. 'Again, it sounds just like home.'

She tipped her head and looked searchingly at him. 'Do you miss it?'

'The hospital? No. The weather? Definitely no—well,

not the cold, anyway. However, I hear the snow's thick
and I imagine they're all skiing every spare minute.'

Sarah eyed him thoughtfully. 'You sound wistful. Will
you miss the skiing?'

'That obvious, huh?' He grinned, a mischievous,
cheeky grin that made her insides flutter. 'Yeah, I'll miss
it. I'm sure I'll find something else to take its place—
and, anyway, Emily isn't too keen. She prefers to swim.'

'There's a good pool in the town.'

'Is there? Do you go?'

She thought of the water and swallowed irrational
panic. 'Not recently. I don't have children.' She held his
gaze steadily. Not any more, at least, she thought, and
prided herself on not flinching. 'I expect Ryan takes his
kids—he'll be able to tell you where it is.'

She was saved any further conversation by Ryan's
arrival. He shook Matt warmly by the hand, recharged
their cups from the coffee-machine, which had gurgled
and burped its way to completion, and sprawled out opposite Matt, filling what was left of the floor with his
outstretched legs.

'How's Emily coping with school? Heard anything?'

Matt held up a hand, as if warding off evil. 'Not a
word. Please, God, she's OK. I'm not calling the
school—no news has to be good news.'

Ryan chuckled. 'She'll be fine. They're very good
there. Evie and Gus love it.'

'Let's hope she does, too.' He drained his coffee, set
the cup down and leant forward expectantly.

Coiled, Sarah thought. Like a spring, or a cat ready
to pounce. She watched him as he chatted to Ryan about
the unit, answering questions here and there, and then
Ryan got to his feet and suggested they went on a grand
tour.

'Want me?' Sarah asked as they headed for the door.

'Sarah, you're always wanted,' Ryan said with a grin, 'but just for now I think I can almost cope.'

She poked her tongue out and debated having another cup of coffee as she listened to them walking off down the corridor to Ryan's running commentary on the layout of the unit.

She had work to do, despite her remarks to Matt. If nothing else there was stock to check and requisition, and after such a hectic weekend it wasn't fair to leave it all to her juniors, quiet or not. All she needed today was someone on the hospital management committee coming round and asking why they'd used so many wrist supports over the past week, and she'd be sorely tempted to take the pad of requisition slips and post it where the sun didn't shine!

Matt followed Ryan, taking in the details of the unit with half his mind while the other half dwelt on Sarah Cooper. Ryan had mentioned her, but more as a colleague than anything. He hadn't touched on her looks. Maybe he hadn't noticed, which wasn't surprising considering how deeply involved he was with his wife.

Matt, though, couldn't get her face out of his mind and he found himself looking for her around every corner, listening for the sound of her voice, waiting for her to reappear.

He wondered how long her hair was. It looked sleek and heavy, a very dark brown that owed nothing to a bottle. It was up, but down it could have been anything from shoulder-length. He wondered what it would feel like, and knew it would be soft and heavy for Emily's was. The thought of this woman's hair threatened to drive him to distraction.

Like her voice. Soft and lilting, no sharp edges or harsh notes—it was made for whispering tender words in a moment of passion. So were her lips, soft and kiss-able, full enough without being pouty, unadorned with lipstick, like early-morning lips.

And her eyes, hazel with a touch of gold, gentle eyes with a hint of sadness—eyes that had seen too much, endured above and beyond the call of duty.

Yes, if he had to find one word to sum her up it would be soft—soft and womanly, with curves in all the right places and not a skinny angle to be seen.

He hated skinny angles.

'This is Resus.'

He jerked his head up and looked around, conscious of how little attention he'd been paying. Hell, he couldn't afford to get distracted like that, someone's life might depend on him paying attention in the next few minutes so that he knew the ropes.

He forced thoughts of the soft and delectable Sarah Cooper out of his mind—for now. He'd have to get to know her, but he had plenty of time. Three months.

Suddenly it didn't seem long enough.

Sarah was uneasy about the quietness. She shouldn't be, she knew. She should just be taking advantage of it to do the mundane routine things like the stock-check and putting that curtain back on the hooks that a drunk had half pulled down over the weekend, but she found she was restless.

Was it because of the unaccustomed quietness, or because of Matt, their new member of staff? He was sup-posedly over in England to study the way trauma units here worked, and he was going to go away with a false impression of how *little* they worked unless something happened, Sarah thought—and then the phone rang.

'Elderly female, hypothermic, suspected fractured femur, on her way in—and the paramedic with her needs looking at. He's been bitten.'

'Bitten?'

Sarah could almost hear the woman on ambulance control shrug. 'So they said. ETA ten minutes.'

'OK, thanks.'

She put the phone down and went to find Ryan. 'Hypothermic lady with a hip on the way in—and she's bitten the paramedic, by all accounts, so I suggest we send her up to Orthopaedics nice and quickly!'

Ryan grinned. 'I think we'll let Matt take his first case—I wonder if she's got rabies?'

'Gee, thanks, I can hardly wait,' Matt murmured, rolling his eyes, and Ryan laughed and slapped him on the back.

'Come on, let's get you a white coat and a stethoscope so you look like a real doctor, and then you can come and play.'

'Wow, I haven't played doctors and nurses for years,' Matt said with a grin. 'Who gets to take their clothes off first?'

'You, if you're not careful,' Sarah quipped, and left them to it, trying not to think about playing doctors and nurses with Matt. Instead she concentrated on playing nurses for real, and prepared a trolley in case they had to rewarm their patient with peritoneal dialysis, warming some saline in readiness.

In the event their patient was only mildly hypothermic, and they wrapped her in a foil blanket, treated her with warmed, humidified air and forty per cent oxygen, and because she was very dehydrated they set up an IV line to dribble in warmed fluids to boost her gently.

While she was waiting for an X-ray they turned their attention to the paramedic, who was clutching his groin and looking pained.

Sarah's eyes widened and brimmed with laughter. 'What on earth did you do to her that she bit you there?' she asked, astonished. 'You must have really upset the poor woman.'

'What? What woman?'

'Mrs Pomfrey—wasn't it her that bit you?'

The paramedic gave a pained chuckle. 'Whatever gave you that idea? It was her dog that bit me—some bloody pit-bull cross, I reckon, from the jaws it had on it. She said it was a terrier—called it Fifi.'

'Really?' Sarah snapped some gloves on and grinned. 'I thought the woman had bitten you—that's what ambulance control said. Oh, well, off with your trousers, let's have a squint at this. Did Fifi get anything vital?'

'Bloody well tried,' he muttered, undoing his zip and sliding his trousers down. Sarah helped him remove them, then the torn boxer shorts, just as Matt came in.

'One chewed paramedic, name of Tom Hallam,' she told him. 'It was a dog called Fifi, by the way, not the patient, who bit him.'

Matt grinned. 'That's a relief. Human bites are usually dirtier than dog bites, but I think our old dear could only have gummed you to death, Tom. What's the damage?'

Sarah swabbed the bloodstained skin and revealed a nasty tear and a couple of puncture wounds just at the top of his left thigh, in the groin area.

'Looks like the extent of it,' she told him.

Matt nodded, checking the area for any other puncture wounds. 'Lucky. A couple of inches to the right and you'd have been singing falsetto. Maybe she thought you were the postman.'

'The vet, more likely—and a couple of inches to the right and the dog would have been in orbit by now,' Tom said with a grin, propping himself up to see the damage. 'Reckon I got away with that quite lightly, considering.'

'Absolutely. I think we need to suture that tear, though, Sarah, if you could give him some local?'

She was already there, drawing up the lignocaine. As she swabbed his thigh and lifted the syringe, Tom caught her wrist, laughter playing in his eyes.

'Anybody says, "Just a little prick," and I'll sue,' he said softly.

She froze for a second, and then the mirth just bubbled over. By the time Ryan came to find out what was going on, she was leaning against the wall, tears running down her cheeks, the half-naked paramedic was doubled up on the couch and Matt was sagging over the foot of it, wheezing.

Matt, speechless, waved a hand at Ryan and hissed something unintelligible. Sarah straightened, struggling to regain her composure, and Tom unwound himself and lay down again with a little groan.

Ryan glanced at the man, now lying flat, and arched a brow at Sarah and Matt. It was enough to set them all off again, and Ryan, shaking his head, walked off in amused disbelief.

It was twenty minutes before they managed to finish off and send the hapless paramedic on his way, still grinning.

They were just on their way to find Ryan for the rest of the A and E tour when the phone rang again, just as the waiting-room doors opened on a great swell of people, all unrelated, all arriving at the same time.

'Told you it was too good to be true,' Sarah said drily. 'Let's see how you cope under pressure.'

Well, was the simple answer. Any fears they'd had about the language barrier and different terminology were swept aside by the sheer volume of work they had to get through.

There were two RTAs, one serious with fatalities and the other a driving instructor and his pupil who had both been caught out by the black ice and had suffered minor whiplash injuries, sliding into the kerb. In between were all manner of walking wounded—what Matt called 'street and treat' cases.

'They walk in off the street, you treat them and send them back out again—hence the term.'

Some of the ones who walked in didn't walk out again, of course. One young man had been driving a tractor with a flail on it, cutting the hedge, and it had tangled in a wire fence. He felt a little stinging cut near his hipbone but ignored it, carried on and finished the hedge.

'I just felt a bit strange at lunchtime and I can feel a little sharp lump—I thought I might have a splinter from the hedge,' he told Sarah.

'Hmm. Can you hang on? I'll just get someone to look at that,' she told him, and went to find Matt who was just finishing up with the whiplashed driving instructor. 'Could you check a patient for me? It doesn't look much but his blood pressure's a bit low and he looks pretty rough—you know how you just feel something's missing in the history?'

'Only too well. What do you know?'

She filled him in, and he went into the cubicle and took a quick look at the 'splinter'. 'Right,' he said calmly. 'I think we need an X-ray to check this out. Just stay there, I'll get them to come to you.'

The mobile X-ray machine was there in seconds, and within a very few minutes they had their answer—a piece of wire from the old fence had penetrated his abdomen and by a miracle had missed all but the smallest vessels.

'He needs the OR,' Matt said quietly. 'Who do I need to speak to?'

'Oliver Henderson's on take today—I'll get his registrar down.'

'I would go for the big guns,' he murmured. 'I just have a feeling.'

It turned out he was right. They heard later that the end of the wire had penetrated the man's aorta, and when they pulled it out he had a massive bleed and needed stitches and a little Goretex patch.

'He was dead lucky there,' Matt said. 'If he'd moved around a lot or changed his clothes or eaten anything much that might have been the end of him.'

'Good job he didn't try and pull it out,' Sarah said with a shudder.

They were in Resus, preparing it for an emergency on the way in, and as she spoke they heard the sirens wail.

'Hello, we're on again,' he murmured.

It might have been difficult, working with a total stranger from another—albeit very similar—country, but for some reason it wasn't. Sarah knew what he was going to ask for, and by and large anticipated it anyway. By the end of that first day they were working in tune, both full of respect and admiration for the other, and well on their way to forming a team.

They were also late, and Matt was concerned about his daughter, so with a grin and a wave he left the department, striding briskly down the corridor, palming the doors out of his way and vanishing.

Sarah was thoughtful. It had been a long time since she'd been so in tune with anyone, if ever. It had been a joy and a privilege to work with Matt, and in between the trauma his wit had coincided with hers.

Ryan found her in the locker room, staring into space. 'Sarah?'

She turned and gave an apologetic smile. 'Sorry, Ryan, did you say something?'

He shook his head. 'Nice guy.'

'Matt? Mmm. Knows his stuff.'

'He's very highly qualified. I don't know what he thinks he'll learn from us, but it will be interesting having him in the department—very interesting.' He shot her a searching look, and then snagged his jacket from his locker.

'I'd better go—Ginny invited him round for supper tonight with Emily and I think I have to go home via a supermarket—I had a shopping list put in my hand this morning as I left home because she doesn't get home from Norwich until six-thirty.' He paused for a moment. 'Don't suppose you want to join us?'

'What—and help you start the meal?'

He grinned. 'Rumbled. So, do you?'

'Want to join you?' She hesitated. It would be nice, and she had nothing else to do tonight and precious little food. Besides, Matt would be there... 'Thanks, Ryan, I will—if you're sure Ginny won't mind the extra mouth to feed.'

He chuckled. 'When has she ever minded feeding you? It's hardly the first time—and, anyway, you can help, like you said.'

She gave a wry grin and watched him go. 'Six OK?' she called after him.

'Wonderful. You can bath the kids.'

She closed her eyes, suddenly tired. Why had she agreed to it?

Because Matt was going to be there.

She felt a shiver of anticipation, and suppressed it.

Matt was a colleague—nothing more, nothing less. Just a colleague.

So they shared a zany sense of humour.

Colleague, she said to herself. Colleague, colleague, colleague.

And, anyway, she wasn't interested in men...

CHAPTER TWO

SPENDING time with Ryan and his children was a refined form of torture. It was, however, a torture Sarah subjected herself to regularly, and Ryan and Ginny seemed to accept her without question. Ryan, of course, knew about Rob and the children, at least in outline, and he knew her well enough to know that his children were safe with her.

How safe she was with them was another question entirely.

She heard the front door open and shut, and Matt's voice filtered up the stairs and into the bathroom. She pulled out the plug and reached for a towel.

'Come on, kids, time to get out and say hello to Emily. Where are your pyjamas?'

Evie, of course, knew where hers were. Gus, of course, didn't have a clue and they had to play hunt the PJs for five minutes in, on and around his bed. The bottoms emerged easily enough from the chaos, but the top was more determined. She ended up lying across the bed, head down, fishing underneath it amongst the clutter he'd hidden there. Finally, though, she located the top.

'Eureka!' Sarah cried and came up victorious, clutching the pyjamas in her hand, her hair dishevelled and on end, to find Matt standing in the doorway with an enigmatic expression on his face. In front of him, wide-eyed and silent, was a little girl with dark hair and huge grey eyes, regarding her steadily as if she were quite mad.

'He lost his pyjamas,' she explained a little lamely, shovelling her hair off her face with one hand and scooting across the bed. 'Gus, here you go, put the top on, please.' She struggled to her feet, straightened her sweatshirt and tried to find a smile.

'You must be Emily,' Sarah said to the child, and she nodded soberly. Gosh, what gorgeous eyes. Like Matt's. 'So, how was school?' she asked her.

For a moment she said nothing, then she sat down next to Gus and sorted out his pyjamas. 'OK, I guess. Mrs Bright's nice. I like her name and she's funny. No, Gus, you put your head through this hole here.'

Sarah hid a smile. Why was it that girls always seemed to end up mothering boys? Even older boys. If things had been different—

She straightened, the urge to smile gone. 'I need to go and help Ryan in the kitchen. Ginny will be home soon and she won't want to have to cook after her long drive.'

'She's back. That's what I came to tell you—and to get out of their way so they can say hi in peace.'

'Oh.' She glanced down at the children, playing happily on the floor with a model farmyard. 'We may as well go down, anyway. We'll just have to interrupt them. I could murder a drink.'

'You and me both,' he murmured. 'I don't think we had time to stop today after that first coffee. I feel totally dehydrated.'

'We'll go and break things up, then, before they get so sidetracked that they forget to cook. I expect your Emily will be tired tonight after her first day at a new school and will need an early night.'

'Not to mention me.'

She grinned. 'You tired? You amaze me.'

He returned her smile with a slow one of his own.

'It's just getting used to the new set-up, although it's not as bad as I thought it might be. It's all surprisingly familiar, really, apart from the odd hiccup when I say CBC instead of FBC.'

She shrugged and started down the stairs. 'Same difference. Full blood count, complete blood count—what's the odds? I find EKG harder. How do you get K from electrocardiogram?' she asked laughingly.

He paused on the top step. 'Search me,' he said with a grin. 'Just so long as you yell when you're lost.'

She stopped on the half landing and turned to look up at him. Heavens, he looked even bigger! 'Don't worry, I'm never lost, and if I was, believe me, I'd yell.' She ran down the last few stairs, conscious of him close behind her, exuding masculine charm in waves.

They found Ryan and Ginny in the kitchen, his hands in the sink scrubbing potatoes, her arms around his waist and her head resting on his shoulderblades.

Ginny straightened and smiled, and Sarah thought she looked tired. 'Hi, there,' Ginny said, and her eyes flicked past Sarah to Matt. 'How did you get on? Ryan says you seemed to fit in very well.'

'He has the same sick sense of humour at least,' Ryan growled from the depths of the sink.

Matt laughed. 'That was just something silly the guy said. It wasn't even that funny, it just struck a note.' He peered in the sink. 'Anything I can do?'

'Yes—make me a cup of tea while Ryan sticks the jacket potatoes in the microwave. He's got fresh salads and cold meat and cheese from the deli counter in the supermarket, so he's got damn all to do. For heaven's sake, don't help him, he's got it easy enough as it is!'

'Ignore her, she's just jealous because she insists on doing it the hard way,' Ryan said with a grin, and then ducked the end of a teatowel Ginny snapped at him.

'Cook, slave,' she ordered, and then ran upstairs to change, leaving Ryan humming happily over his potatoes.

'So, who am I making tea for?' Matt asked.

'Pass. Ginny definitely, and I've never known Sarah say no,' Ryan told him, stabbing potatoes and lobbing them into a dish.

'Absolutely not. Count me in.'

'Unless you'd prefer wine or beer?' he continued, looking at Matt.

'Got any low-alcohol beer?'

'In the fridge. I'll have some too. Sarah?'

She was watching Matt as he stooped over the fridge, his jeans pulled taut over his hips and thighs. 'Tea is fine. I'll make it,' she said absently, and wondered what on earth had got into her that she couldn't seem to stop looking at him. She made tea for herself and Ginny, then took it through to the sitting room, leaving Ryan and Matt alone together.

She needed a minute or two alone, time to think about how she felt and why. It was crazy—must be because they'd worked together all day and were in tune.

So why didn't she feel the same about Ryan, or Patrick, or Jack? Because she worked with them often enough, God knows, and they shared sick jokes and horrendous tragedies and hilarious moments of black comedy.

So why Matt? And why now, after all this time, did she have to choose a man with a child—and not just a child, but a girl, a five-year-old girl with dark hair and solemn eyes, in need of a mother.

Her arms ached, and she hugged them around her waist so they didn't feel so empty. Overhead she could hear Ginny, talking to Ryan's children. She was a step-mother. Her own life had contained tragedy, as had Ryan's, and they were happy.

Clearly it was possible to start again, to find happiness again with someone else.

She tried to remember Rob's face, but she couldn't see it, or hear his voice. Only the voices of the children, and the lusty wail of a new-born baby girl—

'Hi. Which tea's mine?'

'Um—the mug with yellow poppies on it,' she said, and wondered if her voice sounded odd to Ginny or if she'd get away with it.

Nope.

Ginny sat down beside her and laid a hand on her arm. 'You OK?'

She nodded and dredged up a smile. 'Yes, fine. Just a bit tired. I think I'm getting a cold,' she lied.

'Aren't we all? Norwich is hell. I'm thinking of giving up.'

Sarah looked at her in astonishment. 'But you're almost there! You've nearly done your training!'

She shrugged. 'I didn't mean just yet. I want to qualify as a GP, then I can do locum work in the term, but the kids need me. It's all very well Betty and Doug having them occasionally, but they're getting on a bit to have them all the time in the holidays and they need continuity.'

'And you need them,' Sarah added quietly.

'Yes—yes, I do.'

'I can understand that. I need them, too. We're no different in that respect.'

Ginny looked down into her tea and swirled it, her face pensive. 'You could always get married again and have more children,' she suggested tentatively.

Sarah swallowed the tight lump in her throat. 'Yes, I suppose I could. I won't get them back, though.'

Anguish chased across Ginny's weary features, and she reached out to Sarah. 'No, of course not. I'm sorry, I didn't mean to imply they were like tins of beans in a supermarket—just go and buy some more or something. I know you can't get them back. I just thought, if you could fill the void—'

'I know.' Sarah reached out and laid her hand on Ginny's knee for a second. 'I know. Don't worry about me, Ginny, I'm fine.'

'Virginia, do you want me to do all this garlic bread?' Ryan yelled from the kitchen.

She stood up with an apologetic smile. 'Don't run away.'

Sarah didn't run. She sat there, listening to the byplay in the kitchen, the teasing laughter and affectionate ribbing, and tried to remember what it had been like married to Rob.

Very similar, she thought. She couldn't quite remember, though, not clearly. It was almost sad how little she did remember, how much she must have forgotten. It didn't seem to do them all justice, somehow.

Gus came in, trailed by Emily, looking tired but otherwise quite at home. It was amazing how resilient and flexible children were. Gus turned on the television and they sat down cross-legged in front of the screen. Evie ran in then, hugged Sarah in passing and sat down beside them, changing channels until she found something she wanted to watch.

Sensing a squabble brewing, Sarah got to her feet and called the children. 'Shall we go and see if the table needs laying? I think supper's nearly ready.'

'Did I hear Daddy say something about garlic bread?' Evie asked, looking over her shoulder.

'Yes, you did.'

'Oh, yum, I like garlic bread. Come on, you two, let's go and lay the table.'

Sarah followed the headlong dash into the dining room, helped them count the number of places that were needed and then went to find another chair while they set out the cutlery.

Matt was lounging in the kitchen doorway, a beer dangling from his finger, an indulgent smile playing around his lips. He turned to her. 'How long have these two been married?' he asked softly.

She peered past him to where they were wrestling with the corkscrew and giggling, and smiled. 'Just over a year.'

'It shows,' he said drily. 'Shall we start taking things through to the dining room?'

'Good idea.' They loaded up with salads, plates of cold meat and cheese, steaming garlic bread and hot jacket potatoes crisped in the oven, and then went back for Ryan and Ginny.

'If you could bear to drag yourselves apart,' Sarah said from the doorway, 'we've taken everything through. All we need is the wine, one more chair and you two.'

They separated reluctantly, and as Sarah looked at the soft flush on Ginny's cheeks and the possessive glow in Ryan's eyes she thought inexplicably of Matt.

Heat raced through her, taking her breath away.

'You're mad,' she muttered to herself, and turned to find her nose almost on Matt's broad and rather solid chest.

'Excuse me?' he murmured.

'Nothing. Come on, let's eat.'

She went back into the dining room, herded the children onto their seats and sat down amongst them, automatically stopping fights, pouring them half-glasses of

water from the jug and taking two of the four pieces of
garlic bread away from Gus.

'But I like it!' he protested.

'So does everyone else. You have to share—and, anyway, if you have all that, you won't have room for all
the other lovely things.'

The others were seating themselves during this
exchange, and Ryan turned to Matt with a laugh. 'You
can see why we love having Sarah here, can't you? She's
just a natural with them.'

'So I see.'

She could feel his eyes on her, seeing her, all the way
through their meal. She had never felt more watched,
and yet every time she looked up he was looking somewhere else, talking to someone else, spearing a piece of
salad, handing someone something—never looking at
her.

And yet she knew—she just *knew*—that he was.

What she didn't understand was why.

A new SHO on her A and E rotation was attached to
Sarah the next day, so she hardly saw Matt. She missed
him, especially since the young woman was struggling
to deal with the new job.

Sarah had to prompt her to X-ray a person who had
come in, having had a minor shunt in her car and struck
her head on the steering-wheel.

She'd been brought in by a friend, and so ambulance
staff hadn't had a chance to apply a neck brace. Jo
Bailey, the new doctor, asked her how she felt and
treated her like a minor head injury patient, while Sarah,
gradually realising that a cervical examination wasn't
going to be forthcoming, quickly whipped out an X-ray
request form, filled it in and slid it across the desk.

'Dr Bailey, if you could just sign this while I put the

neck brace on, I'll take the patient round to X-Ray for you.'

Dr Bailey, confused and ready to protest, caught Sarah's eye and subsided. She signed the form, handed it back and muttered, 'Thanks.' Sarah slid past her with the patient on the trolley.

'Any time,' she said with a smile and a wink, and stifled a sigh until she was out of earshot.

The result was clear, but it might not have been following a rapid deceleration and subsequent whiplash, and it wouldn't hurt the doctor to learn before it was too late. They had coffee shortly afterwards, and Jo Bailey thanked her again.

'I don't know what I was thinking about. I know you have to check the neck—I must have been cuckoo.'

'There's a lot to remember all at once,' Sarah consoled her, and then they were off again.

Now, however, she was erring on the side of caution, ordering tests that would bleed patients dry and clog up the labs and X-Ray for weeks. Sarah, once again taking over, edited the requests a little, except in cases where she herself felt out of her depth, and then they called on Jack or Ryan.

When Ryan came, Matt came too, and so she got to see him. At one point he paused beside her and, under cover of a screaming child, he glanced at Jo Bailey and raised an expressive brow. 'Is she safe?'

Sarah nearly laughed. 'I have no idea. I suspect not. It may just be nerves, but I think she needs to be attached to someone medical who can stop her using up the region's financial resources single-handed.'

'That bad, huh?'

'Easily. Either that or she forgets to X-ray necks.'

'Holy-moly. She's a liability.'

'Tell me about it. Talk to Ryan—if she works with him she won't come to any trouble.'

'He doesn't need us both.'

Sarah laughed. 'I can nursemaid you—you just use the wrong words.'

He mock-bristled. 'They are not wrong!'

'Just not English. See what he says.'

'I will.' He tapped her on the nose. 'You're prettier than he is.'

She blushed a little but he'd gone, whisked away by another call, and she was left alone with the screaming child and Jo.

Within half an hour they'd swapped, under the pretext of Ryan wanting Jo to see some action in Resus, and Matt was with Sarah. After that last remark she wasn't sure it was a good idea, but after a few minutes she decided it had just been another joke.

She felt perversely disappointed, not that there was much time for flirting. They were rushed off their feet, and she was only too glad to be working alongside someone who knew what they were doing.

She soon got used to him saying 'CBC', 'EKG' and so on and, as on the day before, she found they worked together almost without the need for words.

At one point they were working in Resus alongside Ryan and Jo Bailey, and Sarah was hugely relieved to have Matt opposite her and not Jo. A woman was admitted with severe head injuries, including a massive scalping injury, due to her hair being caught in machinery. Her face had been torn apart, her skull compressed on one side, and there was no chance for her.

'Ouch—bad hair day,' Matt winced, and whistled under his breath. 'Right, let's see if we can stop this bleeding and assess her consciousness level. Do we have a GCS score yet?'

The Glasgow Coma Scale was an international scale used to evaluate the degree of consciousness of a patient, and there was no language barrier. There was no score, either, because the ambulance that had brought her in had had more important things to worry about—like keeping her alive.

Sarah wasn't sure if they would succeed for much longer. They tried, anyway, because she was young and fit and it just seemed a lousy way to go, but it was hopeless.

They shocked her, they injected her with a cocktail of drugs to prompt her heart, but to no avail.

'This is hopeless,' Matt said, shaking his head.

'Want to stop?'

'No, but there's no point going on. She's a corpse, basically. What the hell are we trying to achieve?'

Sarah shut her eyes and sighed. 'You're right. Let's give up. We might even get time for tea if we stop now.'

'Her husband's here,' someone said around the door, and Matt rolled his eyes.

'Wow. I'll go get him, shall I? I expect he'd like to see her—one last fond look.'

They glanced down at the torn and devastated features despairingly. 'Give me ten minutes,' Sarah said.

'You are kidding.'

'No. Do it. Go and talk to him, and get someone to check with me.'

'Goody. This is my first chance to ruin an English family's lives, you realise.'

There was a gasp from the other end of the room, and Sarah looked up to see Jo, staring at Matt in horror.

'Lighten up, kid, it happens all the time,' Matt told her.

'But to joke about it! Don't you have any idea?'

Matt ignored her. 'I guess I'd better wash up.'

'Might be good,' Sarah told him, not even bothering to look at him. She knew just how blood-splattered he must be. She turned her attention, instead, to the wreckage in front of her.

'I'm sorry, there was nothing we could do to save her. Her hair was caught in a machine—she had severe head injuries. There was no way she could have survived.'

The man, about Matt's age, seemed to shrivel. For ages he said nothing, then he looked up, his eyes shocked and far-away. 'Can I see her?'

Matt crossed his fingers discreetly. 'In a while. I'll get someone to come and sit with you and give you some tea—let it sink in a little.'

He slipped back into Resus and did a mild double-take. 'Wow.'

Sarah stood back and looked at her handiwork. 'Will that do?'

She'd obviously washed the woman's face and head, dried the skin and then carefully rearranged the facial features. They looked battered, but the transparent micropore tape holding the skin together was hardly visible, and with the scalp area swathed in drapes the damage was hardly detectable.

Matt was touched. 'That's wonderful. At least he won't have to torture himself for ever with what she might have looked like.'

'Does he want to see her?'

'Oh, yes—don't they always?'

'It does help,' she said softly. 'It makes it real—sometimes too real.'

She turned away, clearing up the mess, swabbing the floor, changing her gown. Jo and Ryan had gone, their patient stabilised and transferred to the ward, and they were alone.

Matt watched her, wondering what to say, how to raise the subject of her loss. 'Do you ever talk about it?'

She stiffened. 'Not often. It doesn't help. It doesn't bring them back. On the other hand it doesn't make it any worse.'

'Hard to see how it could.'

'No. Well, I think we're ready.'

She turned back and her eyes were calm and clear, not filled with tears, as he'd been expecting. She seemed to read his mind.

'I'm OK, Matt. It's all right. You don't have to walk around me on eggshells.'

He nodded, then glanced once more at their patient. 'I'll bring her husband. Stay here, please, so we can restrain him if necessary. I don't want him pulling those towels off and finding the mess underneath.'

She stayed, and while the shocked and grieving husband of their patient said his tearful farewell she stood close and tried not to hear the pain. She didn't allow herself to think of the next few days, weeks, years of his life. Despite what she'd said, things like this brought it all a little too close to the surface.

The man went out, his wife was transferred to the hospital mortuary where the pathologist could do a little more cosmetic work following the post-mortem, and Matt and Sarah went into the staffroom and dropped bonelessly into the chairs.

'Tea?' Ryan offered.

'You bet. Grieving relatives always make me thirsty.'

'Me, too. Nice big mug, Ryan,' Sarah said with a groan, and dropped her head back. 'I could never work in an abbatoir—I just hate the smell of blood.'

'Oh, I love it—did I mention my mother was a vampire?' Matt murmured from the depths of his chair.

'You lot are all so unfeeling!'

They lifted their heads and looked at Jo in astonishment.

'Excuse me?' Matt said mildly.

'Don't you have any thought for what they're going through? The pain, the weeks of grief—'

'Try years,' Matt offered, his voice harsh.

'Years, then. You're all so callous. Your jokes—God, they're sick. You're sick. Fancy seeing that woman and saying she'd had a bad hair day! It's really— Oh, I can't find the words.'

'Common problem down here, finding the right words,' Ryan said in a conversational tone.

'But it's so distasteful!'

'Dying's pretty distasteful,' Ryan told her. 'And, anyway, how do you expect us to grieve with each and every one of our patients and their families? It simply isn't possible.'

'You could try.'

'No—no, you couldn't. It's just a way of dealing with it. It may be sick, but it works, and it's better than burnout.'

'I'm not sure you'd know how to grieve, anyway,' she said disparagingly.

Jack, standing in the doorway where he'd been throughout this exchange, gave a soft snort. 'I think you might find we do. I've lost a son, Ryan's lost his first wife, Patrick's lost his first wife, Sarah's lost her husband and children—I think you'll find, on balance, we know rather a lot about grief. Maybe our way of dealing with it might shock you, but we're still here, years later, saving lives that otherwise would be lost. Not everyone can cope with it. Maybe you'll find you're one of the ones that can't.'

'Maybe.'

She hugged her arms around herself, eyes staring

wildly from one to the other, and a shudder ran through her.

'I'm sorry,' she whispered. 'I had no idea...'

'Poor kid,' Sarah murmured, and went over to her. 'Jo, it's OK. It is nasty. Today hasn't been good. That last case—it was a bit rough. Have a cup of tea.'

'Is that everybody's answer to everything?' Jo said wildly. 'Have a cup of tea? The universal panacea?'

'That's the boy,' Jack murmured, squatting in front of her, mug in hand. 'Here, drink up. You're shocked. You'll get used to it. We all start like this, full of ideals and thinking the old hands are callous. Some of us have been doing it for so long we can hardly remember what it was like to start, but we've all been there. You just take your time.'

He straightened. 'I think you need to work in gently— nice easy cases, nothing too much at first. Why don't you go with Sarah and she can show you a bit of front-of-house stuff in the triage room? Show you how the categories are made up, how the patients are sorted into priorities?'

She nodded, and Sarah slipped an arm round her and gave her a hug. 'You'll do. Drink your tea and come and find me—I'll get out there now, I think there's a bit of a queue after the last two.'

The afternoon passed a little better after that. Nothing else horrendous came in, and Sarah was able to teach Jo some of the fundamentals of processing the patients.

She seemed grateful. She even apologised for being critical, but Sarah brushed it aside, not wanting to get into this conversation. She could tell where it was leading, and she didn't want to talk about Rob and the boys, at least not while she was at work.

She handed over to the next nursing team at four

thirty, and then went into the staffroom for a cold drink, before setting off for home. She mixed the last of the squash and was drinking it when Matt came in and eyed it longingly. 'Is there any more? I could drink the sea dry.'

'No, sorry.' She handed the last of it to him. 'Here, have this.'

He drained it, his throat working, and she watched the stubble-shadowed skin of his jaw with fascination. Then he set the glass down and winked at her. 'Thanks. I needed that. How's the drama critic?'

She smiled, ignoring the flutter in her chest. 'Jo? OK now.'

'She'll learn. Listen, about that swimming pool you told me about yesterday. I—ah—I don't suppose you want to come with us one day this weekend? Show us where it is, have some fun?'

An icy shiver slid down her spine. 'It's easy to find,' she told him evasively. 'I could show you on a map...'

He dug up one of those smiles of his that seemed to undermine her resolve. 'I can find it, I'm sure. I just thought it would be nice for us to have company. Anyway, I actually wanted a favour. I can't take Emily in the men's room any more—she's getting a bit big, but not quite big enough to go into the ladies' room on her own.'

'How do you normally manage?' she asked, ignoring the shiver.

He shrugged. 'Usually I ask a likely-looking mum to give her a hand, but I'd be much happier knowing she was with someone I could really trust—and it can get a bit boring, waiting for her to decide she's had enough. It would be much more pleasant with a civilised adult to talk to.'

His smile was guileless, innocent—and very appealing.

'How about Ryan?' she suggested, still looking for a way out.

'I ask him for so much as it is—and, anyway, I don't want Emily getting too close to Ryan's kids if she's got to leave them in a few months—besides which, if Ginny comes with Ryan I'll feel like a gooseberry again, and if she doesn't it won't help with the changing-room problem.' His smile curled round her again, decimating her defences. 'Are you sure I can't persuade you?'

'Just a swim?' she said suspiciously. 'This isn't a chat-up line?'

He looked surprised, and she felt suddenly foolish.

'Oh, no,' he hastened to assure her. 'I'm here for just three months, and I don't believe in quicky affairs. Trust me, I really meant only a swim, or perhaps a burger afterwards—definitely no strings, I promise.'

And just like that, she found herself talked into it. She even volunteered to be their guide over the coming weekend to show them a little bit of Suffolk—and told herself it was for the sake of the little girl, and nothing to do with a tall, rangy Canadian with a voice like roughened silk and legs that stretched halfway to Alaska...

CHAPTER THREE

SATURDAY morning was cold, bright and just the sort of day for a lovely brisk walk. Sarah wondered if there was the slightest chance she could talk Matt and Emily into it as an alternative to swimming, but she might have known she couldn't.

They arrived as arranged to pick her up at nine-thirty, and when Matt pulled up on the drive in his rental Ford Emily leapt out of the back and ran to the door, just as Sarah opened it.

She looked down at the little girl and her heart sank. She knew, beyond any doubt, that they were going swimming. There was no way Sarah could disappoint her. Her eyes sparkled, her hair was flying and bouncing as she skidded to a halt, and her voice was a breathless squeak.

'Have you got your swimsuit on? I have—I'm all ready. All I have to do is take off my jumper and jeans—'

'Hi, there.' Matt's voice was low and soft and slithered over her nerve-endings, leaving her weak-kneed. 'Emily, darling, slow down. It's too early to be so cheerful.'

So he wasn't a morning person, Sarah thought with a little smile. She opened the door wider. 'Hi. Come in— I've just got to pick up my things.'

They followed her into the hall, and she ran upstairs and picked up the bag from her bed. She'd got it ready earlier, all the while debating whether she could bring herself to do this. Now, it seemed, she had no choice.

She didn't give herself any more time to fret about it, but ran downstairs again and smiled brightly.

'Right, then, shall we go?'

Matt gave her a keen look and she wondered if her false cheer was really that transparent or if she had a smut on her nose.

They arrived at the swimming pool within minutes, and she took Emily through to the changing room. It was, in fact, a communal changing room, with cubicles and family areas, so Matt could have brought Emily by himself. Still, it was too late now to back out, she thought, and, anyway, she might surprise herself and enjoy it.

She always used to, but that, of course, was before—

'Sarah? Are you ready yet?'

She looked down at Emily, bouncing and squirming on the spot, and ruffled her hair. 'Yes, sweets, I'm ready. Come on.'

They held hands and went through the shower together, and the feel of those trusting little fingers curled around hers made Sarah forget what she was about to do. Thank God for the shower, she thought, sticking her head under it so that water ran down her face and disguised the tears. That little hand...

'OK, guys?'

Her breath stopped dead in her chest. Matt was propped against the wall, legs crossed at the ankle, arms folded over a broad chest with a light scattering of hair arrowing down the centre. Water from the shower beaded his skin, glistening in the bright lights and showing off his powerful shoulders.

He shrugged away from the wall, his muscles rippling slightly, and Sarah tried to remember how her feet worked and how to make her breath go in and out. And she'd thought he looked good in *clothes*?

'All set?'

She nodded, swallowing hard and dragging her eyes away from his body. Emily bounced over to him and caught his hand, towing him towards the leisure pool—and Sarah, too, because her hand was still firmly held as well. There were fountains and islands, a crocodile lurking in the shallows, and lots of little children splashing and shrieking and having a wonderful time.

She felt the tension leave her. It was just a swimming pool. She would be fine. They would be fine.

She let them lead her into the water, absently noticing a lifeguard on duty at the side of the pool, watchful eyes scanning the area, whistle at the ready to halt any silliness. Emily slipped her hand free and dived into the water, turning onto her back and beckoning Sarah.

'Catch me!'

She turned over and sped off, slippery as an eel, darting through the water and disappearing behind an island.

'It's deep there,' she began worriedly, but Matt just grinned.

'She swims like a fish. She's fine. You go that way, I'll go the other.'

She went, but slowly, and wasn't surprised to hear a little shriek and find Emily in Matt's arms, giggling and splashing him. He released the child and followed her, disappearing under the surface and tickling her. Sarah decided they could both swim a lot better than she could, and so she left them to it, wallowing on her back in the shallows, elbows propped on the shelving 'beach', watching them.

Emily certainly seemed to be having fun—and so was she, Sarah discovered to her amazement. Matt appeared, swarming over the crocodile and sitting astride it, grinning. 'Mick Dundee, ma'am, at your service,' he said in a lousy Australian accent.

She laughed and splashed him. 'Idiot.'

He grinned, unabashed by her put-down, and settled beside her, legs outstretched, scanning the water and checking Emily. They chatted idly, his eyes never leaving Emily, and Sarah thought what a good and devoted father he was.

They were interrupted by a disembodied voice, calling for everyone's attention and warning them that the wave machine was going to be switched on. 'Everybody behind the steps, please. All non-swimmers stay behind the islands.'

'Will Emily be all right?' Sarah asked worriedly. 'Shouldn't she be back here?'

'She's fine. She loves wave machines. Come on in.' He stood up and held out a hand to her, but she scooted further up the beach and shook her head.

'No, I'll stay here. You go to Emily.'

He hesitated, then nodded and turned, wading out towards his daughter. He reached her just as Sarah felt a pull on the water around her legs, a current, like an undertow—

She scrambled to her feet and went and sat on a low wall overlooking the pool, fighting the waves of panic that threatened to swamp her. Was that what it had been like, to feel the suck of the water, dragging you down?

Her arms wrapped around her waist, hugging her sides, and a shudder ran through her. She was rocking, she realised, and a woman paused beside her and studied her anxiously. 'Are you all right, my love?' she asked gently.

Sarah forced a smile and made herself sit still. 'Yes, I'm fine. Just a bit cold, but I hate the waves.'

'Me, too. Here, borrow this towel for a moment. My kids won't mind.'

She wrapped a soft, warm towel round Sarah's shoulders and sat beside her, chattering inconsequentially. Gradually the shudders died away, and the sound of the laughing, happy children penetrated the fog of panic surrounding her.

She looked up and saw Matt and Emily, surfing up the beach. As they turned to go back towards the deep end, a boy ran along the side of the pool and slipped.

He landed flat on his back, his head hit the edge with a sickening thud and he slid over the side into the deepest part of the water—right by the gaping maw of the wave machine. Matt must have seen because he turned and disappeared beneath the water, heading for the spot where the boy had slipped under.

'No!' She leapt to her feet, dropping the towel, and ran down the side as the lifeguard blew a whistle. She could see Matt being sucked down after the boy, reaching for him, grabbing him, both of them pulled against the mesh guard over the wave machine. Panic clawed at her again, choking her, and hot tears stung her eyes. 'Help them!' Sarah screamed. 'Get them out!'

'Everybody clear the pool,' a voice said over the loudspeakers, and a lifeguard dived in beside Matt and helped him bring the boy to the surface.

The wave machine must have been switched off, she realised dimly as Matt and the lifeguard swam up to the beach and carefully slid the boy up onto the tiles.

Matt was looking around, searching for someone, and caught her eye. 'Sarah, come here. I need your help.'

She stood there, rooted to the spot, unable to move as relief washed over her. He was alive. He hadn't drowned—

'Sarah!'

His voice galvanised her, and she crossed quickly to him, pushing through the crowd that was now forming.

'I've got a first-aid certificate,' someone was saying.

'It's all right, he's a doctor,' she said absently, and knelt down on the other side of the boy, facing Matt. 'He hit his head.'

'I know. It's starting to bleed, but I want to check his spine. I think he winded himself, so hopefully there isn't any water in his lungs—the wave machine would have sucked it out anyway. Check his airway.'

She did, by lifting his jaw without touching his neck, functioning on autopilot.

'Airway's fine, but he's not breathing.' She bent over and closed her mouth over the boy's nose and mouth, breathing firmly into him. His lungs seemed to resist the inflation and she wondered how badly he'd winded himself. Sometimes if the air was knocked right out of the lungs they found it almost impossible to inflate again.

'Any joy?' he asked her.

'Maybe. His pulse is strong.'

'Daddy? Matt?'

'It's OK, sweetheart—just sit down and wait for me, darling, there's a good girl. He's going to be all right.' His hand continued to slide down the boy's spine, feeling each vertebra for any possible abnormality.

'Seems OK—it was a pretty flat landing but I want to be sure.' He turned to the lifeguard who was trying to disperse the crowd. 'Do you have a backboard?'

'Sure. I'll get it.'

'Why do they want a blackboard?' someone asked.

'A backboard, stupid—I think he's broken his back,' was the reply. 'I expect he'll be paralysed.'

Matt took the boy's arms and lifted them up and out, pulling the chest wall up as Sarah breathed into his mouth. Just then the boy coughed, dragged in a great gasp of air and started to cry, curling up his legs and wrapping his arms around his waist.

'He's not paralysed,' the first one said, sounding almost disappointed.

The rest of the crowd cheered. Sarah ignored them, concentrating her attention on the boy and comforting him by holding his hand while Matt checked his pupils and spoke to him, asking his name, the day of the week, how he'd got to the pool that morning—anything to check that he knew who and where he was.

'He seems lucid. I think he's been lucky. Darren, are your parents here?'

'No—I'm with my mates.'

Matt lifted his head. 'Darren's friends about?' he asked the crowd.

Two boys stepped forward, looking worried. Matt turned to the lifeguard. 'Can we get rid of the rest of this lot? If we can slip him onto the backboard and lift him out of the way, they can all carry on and we won't have an audience. We need to call an ambulance—I want to get this head checked and stitched and make sure everything else is OK. Do you boys know his home phone number?'

'Yeah.'

An official was there by then, hovering and making notes, and he took the boys off to contact Darren's parents, with Matt's instructions that they were to proceed directly to the hospital.

A few minutes later Darren was removed in the ambulance, the 'beach' had been swabbed down and the place was back to normal. Sarah, though, felt as if she'd lost ten years off her life.

Matt took her arm and towed her towards the changing rooms, Emily tucked in against his side. 'Emily, you go with Sarah and get changed, I'll see you out the front in a few minutes. I want to follow him to the hospital.'

His eyes were keen, searching Sarah's face, and she avoided them. She nodded and shepherded Emily to the lockers, retrieved their clothes and went and changed.

'I don't have my underwear!' Emily wailed, searching through her things. 'I forgot!'

Sarah dredged up a smile. 'Just put your clothes on without, and we'll go home and change you after your daddy's checked things at the hospital. OK?'

Emily nodded and struggled into her jeans, trailing the hems in a puddle and getting stuck halfway down one leg, with her wet foot refusing to release the fabric.

Sarah helped her, towelled and combed her hair and then quickly finished herself off, before gathering their wet things up and pushing them into a bag. 'All set?'

Emily nodded, and together they went out, Emily still wriggling one foot into a shoe, to find Matt waiting, pacing the foyer. They all but ran to the car, and once at the hospital he told Sarah to entertain Emily while he checked Darren.

She took the little girl into the staffroom and got her a glass of squash, then hunted around to see if there was anything to eat.

'Oh, look, a box of chocolates. They must be from a patient. Here, have one.'

She had three in the end before Matt appeared with a smile in the doorway.

'OK?'

'Yes, he's fine, he's gone home with a head injuries card just in case, but I'm sure he'll be fine.'

He helped himself to a chocolate, then looked at the other two. 'Right, how would you like to go and play with Evie and Gus while I take Sarah for a coffee?'

'OK. I've got no underwear on—I forgot.' She wrinkled her little nose, and he laughed and hugged her head against his side.

'I'm sure Evie will have some she can lend you, just this once. Come on.'

'I don't really need a coffee,' Sarah told him, wondering how long it would be before she could go home, crawl into a corner and forget about the last few hours. It had all been too much, and she really didn't feel up to making small talk or, worse still, rehashing the events.

She just wanted to forget.

Matt, though, didn't seem to be about to let her. 'I need one,' he told her, 'and I could use some company.'

He wouldn't be put off, Sarah realised—not, at least, without making him suspicious and then having to face the ordeal of explaining. She subsided. It was only coffee. She could manage.

They dropped Emily off at Ryan's, then drove round the corner to her house just two streets away. 'Why are we here?' she asked him, confused, as he pulled up on her drive.

'Because I think it's time you and I had a chat, and I don't think you're going to want to talk about this in public.'

'Talk about what?' she asked cautiously.

'About your reaction to the wave machine and to that boy's accident.'

She swallowed and looked away. 'Why do we need to talk about it?'

'We don't. I think you do, and I'm here, and I've got broad shoulders.' He opened his door, got out and went round and opened hers, waiting until she swung her legs round and stood up. His arm circled her waist, pulling her out of the way of the door, and then he shut it, led her to the front door, took her keys from her icy fingers and let them in.

'Kettle?'

'In the kitchen. I'll do it.'

He followed her, sitting at the table and waiting patiently while she fiddled about and wondered how to avoid what was coming. Finally, she felt his hands close over her shoulders and ease her gently aside. He finished off the coffee, handed her one and led her back to the table, pushing her down into the other chair. Then he waited.

She stirred her coffee, casting around for a place to start. In the end she just started at the beginning, which was as good a place as any.

'They went fishing. It had been raining heavily and Rob said the river would be a bit too full and fast to catch anything, but he'd promised the boys he'd take them, so he did. I stayed at home and rested. I'd just lost a baby. I'd always known it would happen, but it hit me harder than I had thought it would. Rob took the boys out to give me some peace.'

Her voice sounded flat and curiously lifeless even to her own ears. She curled her fingers round the mug, drawing warmth from it.

'They didn't come back. I started to worry in the afternoon because the boys were only two and four and got bored easily. I thought maybe Rob had taken them to a funfair or something. There'd been a circus and Toby had wanted to go on the big wheel. Anyway, later that day I called the police and told them where they'd gone fishing.

'They found his car, parked where I thought it would be, but no sign of them. They found some of their gear, though, near the little wooden jetty where they used to sit, and rang the coastguard.'

She chased a bubble round the top of her coffee with a finger, heedless of the heat. 'There'd been a rip tide.

The Severn's known for them. It happens when the out-
going river in flood meets an incoming tide. A wall of
water had come up the river and swept them off the jetty.
They were found ten miles apart over the next two days.'

She looked up and met Matt's clear, steady gaze.
'That's why I don't like swimming much.'

His hand covered her wrist, warming it, giving her
strength. 'It was the wave machine, wasn't it?' he said
flatly.

'The pull. I thought how the boys must have felt, being sucked under...'

Her hand shook and the coffee spilled over, puddling
on the table. 'Damn.'

She got up to fetch a cloth, and found herself in Matt's
arms, cradled against the soft wool of his jumper. His
hands felt like a shield, sheltering her, warding off the
terrible memories, but they came anyway.

'I went and saw them,' she told him. 'Rob had a
scrape along his cheek, but the boys just looked small
and pale and very still, as if they were asleep...'

She didn't even realise she was crying, but his arms
tightened, drawing her closer to his warmth, and under
her ear she could hear the steady beat of his heart. 'I
thought—when you were sucked down—'

'Shh. I was fine. I knew they'd turn it off.'

'They might not have.'

'They'd seen him. They were already moving.'

She sniffed and tipped her head, meeting his eyes. 'It
was just too close for comfort. That boy—'

'I'm sorry. I wish I hadn't taken you. I knew your
husband and children had drowned—Ryan told me, just
very briefly. I didn't think a swimming pool would
worry you, otherwise I would never have suggested it.'

'I nearly didn't go.'

'I'm sorry it turned out like this. I don't know what to say.'

She smiled wanly. 'Don't say anything. I'm all right. Nothing that happens can make it any worse, it's never very far away.'

She eased out of his arms and got the cloth, blotting up the coffee. 'That's it, really. It was five years ago, in August. Sometimes it seems like yesterday, and at other times I feel as if I've been alone for ever.'

She rinsed the cloth and hung it over the tap, then looked down the garden. It was drab and wintry, the branches of the trees all bare, the grass mossy and covered in leaves. 'I ought to get out there and do something with that,' she said absently.

'I'll give you a hand if you like.'

'Would you? What about Emily?'

'She'd help, too. She might have fun.'

'She might have more fun playing with Gus and Evie,' Sarah said realistically.

'I'll ask Ryan if they're OK to keep her, but if not she can bundle up warm.'

'Use my phone—it's in the hall.'

She put the mugs in the dishwasher while he rang Ryan, and then went out to him as he cradled the receiver.

'Well?'

'They're fine with that. I could do with some old clothes, though. Want to come back to the flat with me?'

'I'm OK on my own,' she assured him.

'So am I—that doesn't mean I like it, necessarily. It can be a bit lonely over here without any of my friends and family.' He gave a crooked and beguiling grin. 'I just thought it would be nice to have some company, but you don't have to come if you don't want to.'

She shrugged. What harm would it do? Anyway, if she saw his flat she could picture him in it—

'OK.'

They went via a DIY superstore and picked up some gardening gloves for him, and then he pulled up outside a tall Victorian house near the back of the hospital.

It was funny, Sarah thought, how much bigger he seemed in the confines of the hallway. They went upstairs and through the front door of the flat, which opened straight into the living room. Down a passage she could see a bathroom and kitchen, and off the living room were two other rooms—bedrooms, she assumed.

It was clean and tidy, but a little basic. The furniture was typical rental stuff, chain-store velour well past its sell-by date, uncoordinated curtains and carpets, too few scatter cushions, and yet it had a homely feel.

Matt looked around, seeing it with her eyes, perhaps? 'It's nothing special but it'll do us. It's only for a couple of months, after all.'

'It's fine. It's got nice views from the window.'

He stood behind her, looking over her shoulder and making her oddly aware of his closeness. 'I hardly seem to have time to look out of the window,' he said quietly. 'We only seem to be here in the dark.'

She turned, moving slightly away to give herself a little room. 'Do you regret coming to England?'

He searched her eyes for a long moment, then shook his head. 'No. No, I don't regret it. It's a little odd sometimes, not having all my things around, but, no, I don't regret coming here. There's a lot to learn,' he added, and she had the strangest feeling he wasn't talking about the job.

Which was silly, because what else would he be talking about?

He went into the nearest bedroom and stopped in his tracks. 'What the hell—?'

'What is it?'

'The ceiling's down—there's water all over the place. The bed's soaked.'

He came out and went into the other room, and swore freely.

She followed him in and saw chunks of plaster coving lying across the bed in the far corner.

'Thank God she wasn't in bed,' Sarah said faintly.

Matt was white-faced and grimly silent. 'She could have been killed,' he muttered.

'But she wasn't.'

He turned to her, his eyes tracking over her face as if looking for an answer. Water dripped steadily, splashing onto the sodden carpet. 'What the hell are we going to do?'

'Ring the landlord.'

He picked up the phone and punched in a number, then sighed harshly. 'Answerphone,' he growled, then after a pause he spoke into the receiver, giving brief details, and hung up. 'We'll have to move into a hotel,' he said, looking round in disbelief. 'The place is trashed. I'd better pack and warn the people downstairs.'

'I'll go and talk to them, you pack.'

She ran down and knocked on the door, but there was no reply. She went back just as another chunk of ceiling collapsed with a crash.

'That's it, I'm out of here. We'll go and collect Emily and try and find somewhere for the night.'

'It'll take more than a night, Matt. It'll be days— weeks—before this place is straight. There must have been a burst pipe in the roof.'

He stabbed his hands through his hair and sighed again. 'Look, can we go and get Emily and tell Ryan what's happened? He might have an idea where we could stay for a while until this is sorted. Then maybe later he could give me a hand to pack all our stuff and get it out.'

They struggled down the stairs with the suitcases containing all the contents of the bedrooms, and then he went back up, tried the landlord again and found a stopcock in the kitchen. 'I wonder if this turns off that pipe?' he suggested.

It seemed it didn't. 'The leak must be from the flat upstairs—it's empty at the moment,' he told her. 'Oh, well, there's nothing more we can do. Let's go.'

They found the O'Connors up to their eyes in balloon animals, toy dogs and suchlike, made from long sausage-shaped balloons that stayed put when they were bent and twisted. The kids were having a whale of a time, trying to make them, and Ryan and Ginny left them to it and went into the kitchen with Matt and Sarah so they could fill them in about the flat.

'That's horrendous,' Ginny said, wide-eyed, when Matt mentioned the coving, lying across Emily's little bed. 'Thank God she wasn't asleep in it!'

'Don't.' A shudder went through him. 'Anyway, listen, I need to find us a hotel somewhere for the next couple of nights.'

'I'd invite you here, but we've got friends coming later for a day or two,' Ryan said, stabbing his hands through his hair. 'I wonder if we can put them off?'

'No, no, I wouldn't hear of it. I'll find somewhere.'

Ginny turned to Sarah. 'Haven't you got a spare room they could have, just until they find somewhere?'

She felt everyone's eyes swivel to her. 'If you could put them up for a night or two, that would give Matt time to find something more permanent,' Ginny continued persuasively.

'Yes—yes, of course,' she said, automatically agreeing.

'Well, that would be wonderful, just for a night or two. Thanks.'

'Actually, I've got three empty bedrooms,' Sarah said into the lull. 'They're not doing anything and I haven't got anyone booked to stay. In fact,' she continued, wondering if her mind was totally out to lunch, 'there isn't any reason why you shouldn't stay for the whole of your time here—if you wanted to. It's clean and warm and comfortable, it's handy for Emily's school and Gus and Evie—it's up to you. There's even room in the garage for your car.'

He said nothing, just watched her for a moment until she felt she'd put him on the spot and made it difficult for him to refuse.

'That's silly,' she rushed on. 'I expect you'd much rather have your own place, but if you wanted to stay just until you found something—'

'No. Not at all, but it's a lot to take on. Did you mean it?'

Here was her chance to back out, but for some perverse reason she didn't take it. 'Yes, I meant it,' she told him. 'Like you said, it can get a bit lonely by yourself. It would be nice to have some company for a change, and it might help you with Emily's babysitting when you're on call.'

A slow smile spread over his face. 'If you're really sure, then it would be wonderful. Thank you. I'm really grateful. I'll pay you, of course.'

Sarah thought of the charities she supported regularly and how they would benefit, and smiled. 'Done. We'll finalise it later.'

Ginny beamed from one to the other. 'Well, that's

marvellous. The kids will be thrilled to have Emily so close.'

Ryan glanced at his watch. 'Listen, why don't you two go and move all the stuff while we keep Em, and then you can come and get her and she can help unpack. I'd say she could stay longer, but these friends will be here soon.'

'She could come with us now.'

'And go back in that flat, with the ceiling coming down?'

Matt nodded grimly. 'You're right. We'll be back in about an hour. Thanks.'

It took them a little over an hour, but they'd got everything out just as the landlord arrived.

'You're leaving,' he said, sounding surprised.

'Yes—I don't want my daughter in danger.'

'I've got another flat I can move you to,' he began, but Sarah cut across him.

'It's all right, they're coming to stay with me.'

'But there's a lease—'

Matt laughed. 'You really think I'm going to stay after this? I'll be expecting a refund of overpaid rental, and my deposit returned. You can contact me at the hospital. I'll be in touch.'

'But I'm entitled to notice!'

'So claim off your insurance.'

They left him there, pondering the disagreeable nature of his tenants, and went back to Sarah's, unloaded the boxes and cases off the back seat and then, while she cleared a cupboard in the kitchen for his food, he went to collect Emily.

They arrived a few moments later, and Emily bobbed into the kitchen, her eyes sparkling. 'Are we really going to stay with you, Sarah?' she asked excitedly.

Sarah sat back on her heels and smiled. 'Yup.'

'Oh, wow, goodee!'

She threw herself into Sarah's arms, and they closed reflexively round the little girl, cradling her close. It felt good to hold her—almost too good. She dropped a kiss on her head, and noticed that her hair smelled of chlorine. She ruffled it affectionately. 'We need to give you a bath, sweets. You smell of the swimming pool.'

'You can smell it here, too, if I lick my arm—see?' She licked her arm and held it under Sarah's nose. Sarah dutifully sniffed and nodded.

'So you can. Amazing. Right, let's go up and have a look at the bedrooms, and you can choose which one you'd like, and then you can have a bubble-bath while we sort out your clothes and unpack them, OK?'

Emily skipped up the stairs ahead of Sarah, darting in and out of all the rooms.

She stopped, as Sarah had known she would, in the little bedroom with pretty, flowery wallpaper and curtains. The bed was covered in a lovely patchwork quilt, and the window looked out over the garden. She spun round and looked up at Sarah, her eyes wide.

'May I have this one?'

Sarah smiled. 'Of course.'

'Where's Daddy going to be?'

She pointed across the landing. 'In there. It's the biggest, after mine.'

'And he is big, isn't he, so he'd need it? Poor Daddy—if he was smaller he could have had this room.'

Sarah suppressed her smile at the thought of Matt in the single bed surrounded by flowers. 'I don't think you'll find he minds that room.'

'OK.'

Matt put her case on the floor and instructed Emily to find her pyjamas and wash-things, and they went into his room.

Matt pushed the door to and met her eyes. 'Are you sure about this, Sarah? It won't worry you, having a child in the house?'

She shook her head, touched by his thoughtfulness. 'Oh, no. I often have children in the house. That's why I bought this four-bedroomed house when I moved up here. I'd got the insurance money from Rob and the children, and I wanted somewhere where my family could come and stay.' And, anyway, she could have added, having you here is infinitely more disturbing than Emily could ever be.

He looked away, studying the room with more attention than it really merited. 'She seems very fond of you already.'

Was that a warning? She decided to answer the concern she'd thought she detected in his voice, just in case.

'She's a delightful child. I'm fond of her—but I also know she's going home again, so I won't let her get too close, for her sake as well as mine.' She laid her hand on his arm. 'Don't worry, Matt. I know how to look after myself. I've been doing it for years. Now, why don't you unpack and put Em in the bath while I go and hunt up something for supper?'

'We'll have to sort out finances.'

She nodded. 'OK. Tell you what, why don't you give me what you were paying for the flat, and we can take turns cooking and share the housekeeping—OK?'

He nodded, and she went downstairs and opened the freezer. Good. That would give her a few hundred pounds towards the SIDS charity, which would buy a few baby monitors. She'd never lost a child to a cot death, but she'd lost the boys and it didn't take much imagination to know how nervous parents who'd lost a baby to SIDS would feel with the next baby. This money from Matt would help to reassure some of them in those difficult early weeks.

And he was going to help her in the garden.

Happier by the minute with her new house guests, she took some chicken fillets out of the freezer and set about making supper.

CHAPTER FOUR

IT WAS odd having them in the house. True, Sarah had had friends and family to stay many times, but usually when she wasn't working. It felt strange, waking up to the sound of the shower running in the main bathroom, and hearing Matt moving around in the room next door while she was getting ready for work.

She found she was always conscious of him, and more than once her unruly imagination strayed into dangerous territory. Of course, since their swim it had lots more ammunition to arm her fantasies, and she found herself unable to meet his eye on occasion for fear he'd read her mind.

And then there was Emily. She was delightful, but having her in the house was definitely like a two-edged sword. She was untidy, sometimes wilful and possessed of a delicious sense of humour—a legacy, no doubt, of her father.

She reminded Sarah almost painfully of Toby, her oldest son. He'd been untidy and quick-witted, too, and there was something about her expression that brought back memories of him.

Not that they looked at all alike. Her boys had been the spitting image of Rob, fair-skinned redheads with bright blue eyes, whereas Emily had dark hair and her father's dark grey eyes. It was just certain moments, little fierce frowns when concentrating, the rolling belly laughs—and the temper.

Emily, she discovered, had a temper.

So did Matt, and although he kept it in check in front

of Emily sometimes he'd come down after a 'conversation' with her and punch his fist into a cushion to let off steam.

She remembered doing the same when the boys were around. She supposed every parent did it—except for the ones who didn't. They hit their kids instead.

They had a steady stream of NAIs through A and E. Any Non Accidental Injury to a minor had to be notified to the duty social worker if there were reasonable grounds for suspicion, and in any event after the third occasion, no matter how plausible the parents' explanations were.

They were the cases Sarah hated. Having lost her own children, she couldn't understand how anyone could wilfully damage their child, no matter how aggravating the child might have been.

That was where Matt came in handy. After one particularly nasty case where a girl had brought in her younger brother because the father had just started on him as well, Sarah sat down in the sitting room with Matt after Emily was in bed and thrashed out the case with him.

'I just find it so tragic that she was upset because she'd squealed on her father. After all he'd done to her, how could she be so loyal?'

Matt shrugged. 'Kids often are. Their parents may be the very dregs of the earth, but they're their parents. It seems to be true—blood is thicker than water, or all these kids would a lot safer because they'd say something much sooner.'

'Unless they'd been threatened.'

'That's usually sexual abuse.'

'What's the difference? It's a violation, whichever.'

He shook his head thoughtfully. 'I'd rather be hit than raped.'

'Repeatedly? Burned with cigarettes? Whipped with bare electric wires?'

'It's a tough choice. Thankfully it's only theory and I don't have to choose. My parents were wonderful. Any parenting skills I have I get from them.'

Sarah nodded agreement. 'Mine were, too, but I learned a lot from the boys as well. They train you, if you listen.'

Matt regarded her in silence for a moment. 'You must miss them.'

She held his gaze. 'Every day. Not Rob now, so much. It's funny. When you meet you think you couldn't ever love anyone else, but when you get right down to it, it's your children who are irreplaceable. Lovers, husbands, wives—they're easier to replace. Time heals. You can always fall in love again if the right person comes along, but you never get your kids back—however you lose them.'

Something flickered in his eyes, and he looked away. 'You could always have other children. You're only thirty or so, aren't you?'

'Yes—but I'd need a partner, and I don't have one.'

'Anyone on the menu?'

Her imagination ran riot again, but she quelled it. He'd already told her he wasn't in the market for an affair. 'No, not really.'

'I'm surprised. You're a beautiful woman. I would have thought they'd be queuing up.'

She laughed a little tightly. 'Hardly. Who wants to take on someone with my history? Talk about a desperate widow.'

'Are you? Desperate?'

She laughed again and got up, pacing to the window. 'No, of course not,' she said a little too quickly. 'I'm quite happy like this, alone.'

'Are you?'

He was still sitting down but she was suddenly terribly aware of him. 'Aren't you ever tempted to have an affair?'

She turned slowly, wondering if she'd misunderstood him all along. 'Is that a proposition?'

He laughed and threw up his hands. 'No! I told you, I don't go for quicky affairs and short-term relationships, and I'm off again soon. I just wondered if you'd ever been tempted.'

She shook her head, her panic subsiding to leave something curiously like disappointment in its wake. 'No. I never have and I doubt if I ever will. It's not my thing, either. I'm strictly monogamous. Rob's the only man I've ever been to bed with.'

She went back to her chair, curling up and reaching for the TV remote control. 'What's on?' she muttered, flicking through the channels, hoping for something to distract him from his relentless pursuit of the details of her private life. She was telling him things she'd never told anyone except Rob—talking about their personal relationship in a way that was quite foreign to her.

How did he do it? He ought to work for the police—he'd extract confessions without the criminals even being aware of what he was up to. She flicked past another soap, a documentary on inner-city crime and a sports quiz, then went back to the soap.

'Why not just tell me to butt out?' he said quietly.

She sighed, flicked off the set and glanced across at him. 'OK. Butt out.'

'Sorry.'

His smile was gentle, apologetic, and it did crazy things to her heartbeat. She looked away again hastily.

'Did you love him very much?'

Did she? 'Yes, of course,' she replied. 'He was a wonderful husband and father.'

'And you've never been tempted by another man?'

Until Matt had strolled into her life, the answer had been a definite 'no'. Now it was much more complicated, but she could hardly tell him that, could she?

'Not tempted enough to do anything about it,' she said truthfully after a pause.

'What a waste,' he murmured. 'You should be married with children.'

'I was married with children. Unfortunately they didn't come with any guarantees about mortality.'

'No one ever does,' he said quietly. 'Or permanence, come to that.'

'Tell me about your wife,' she said, turning the tables on him.

He shrugged. 'She was a career-woman. She was not pleased to say the least, when Emily appeared on the scene. It didn't take her long to decide that she didn't want to be a mother.'

'Does she see Emily ever?'

He shook his head. 'Look, I really don't want to talk about her. Let's just say she isn't part of our lives any more and leave it at that.'

'Does Em talk about her?'

'Not often.'

'Do you still love her?'

'My wife?' He snorted. 'After the way she abandoned us? You have to be kidding.' He jackknifed out of his chair and strode to the door. 'I think I'll turn in now, I'm tired. It's been a long day again. I'll see you in the morning.'

Sarah watched him go, then shrugged. So she'd touched a nerve. Fine, he'd touched plenty in the last week or so. She rang a friend about a charity dinner she

was helping to organise, and then contacted another
friend about the forthcoming house-to-house collection
for which she had been volunteered.

Maybe if she kept herself busy they wouldn't have
such cosy chats in the evening—and then they wouldn't
have to answer each other's intrusive questions. That
might make things easier—a lot easier. Especially if her
mind was going to continue to run riot every time he
said the word 'affair'!

Matt lay and stared at the bedroom ceiling and wondered
why on earth he'd agreed to live here with Sarah. OK,
the offer had come at a time when he was desperate, but
it was very unwise, all things considered. He really
didn't want to get involved with her and yet he was
drawn to her. He'd wanted to get closer, but this close?
This was too cosy, too intimate—too dangerous.

He had to work with her for three months, whatever
happened. He didn't need to compromise that, but his
damned hormones wouldn't leave him alone.

He played their conversation back over again, and
found himself absurdly pleased that she had only had
one lover. It proved something about her, something
about her constancy and the value she put on important
details rather than the fleeting needs of her body.

She must have needs. Everyone had needs.

Hell, if she didn't she could have some of his! He had
more than he knew what to do with at the moment. He'd
have to find something to do with himself in the eve-
nings, but it was difficult with Emily to look after and
get to bed early. It meant he was hanging about from
about seven onwards, when he wasn't on call, with nothing to do.

He'd go and buy a laptop tomorrow and settle down
to work on his book. After all, he needed to earn a living

and chasing Sarah Cooper, however tempting, wouldn't pay the rent. Her rent.

He frowned. She was charging him plenty, too, and although he didn't resent it, exactly, he did wonder if she was in financial difficulties. After all this was a big house to run on a nurse's salary, even at the top end. OK, so it had been paid for by her husband's life assurance, she'd said, but even so.

Her car was fairly modest, too, several years old although well cared for, and the furnishings in the house were carefully maintained. Was she struggling?

He wondered about it until he fell asleep, a book lying unheeded across his chest and the bedside light still on...

'Major incident report coming in—stand by, everyone. RTA on the A140 south of Scole—several vehicles involved. We may need to send a team.'

They all stopped to listen to Jack, and then quickly finished the cases they were dealing with until more news came in. It was bad, predictably. They left their patients and went to the briefing.

'I want a team—Patrick, will you come, please? And, Sarah, I think—and, Matt, do you want to go for experience? See how we do it here? I'm sure you'll be found a use for.'

'Too right,' Patrick muttered, shrugging out of his white coat and reaching for a reflective jacket. 'You come with me and hold my hand—I hate doing this.'

'Ooh, duckie,' Matt said with a grin.

'Can't you ever be serious?' Jo Bailey wailed. She looked panic-stricken, and Sarah hoped Jack didn't expect too much of her. She was better than she had been, but she wasn't what you could call a quick study, and out there on a busy road, with all hell breaking loose, she'd be a downright liability.

Please, God, Sarah thought, don't let Jack decide she needs the experience.

He didn't. He decided to keep her there to deal with as many of the patients already waiting as she could manage, under Ryan's eagle eye. Sarah privately thought he'd have his work cut out.

Those who were going quickly handed over any unfinished patients to the others. They were just about done when Ryan called for their attention.

'Right, more details,' he told them. 'There's a chemical spillage, so take protective gear and don't take any stupid risks. Sounds like hydrofluoric acid, but there's some doubt. If it is, let the fire brigade tell you when it's safe to go in, and don't tack yourselves onto the casualty list. We'll have enough to do.'

'Pity, I could do with a few days off,' Patrick quipped, which earned him a black look from Jo.

'Report back and keep us posted,' Ryan said as they left. 'I want to know what the chemical is stat so we can organise a treatment plan. Whatever it is, it's liquid. Just in case it is HF, I'll get some calcium gluconate lined up ready—take some hydrofluoric acid burn jelly with you to apply to minor wounds in transit, and calcium gluconate ten per cent to soak dressings with. And remember, flush everyone and everything copiously with water for five minutes.'

'Only five?' Sarah asked. Usually it was twenty or even more.

'Just to wash off the surface chemical. Only the calcium gluconate will make a difference after that. It's not like other chemical burns. Take syringes so you can inject it subcutaneously into any burns you're concerned about, but the priority has to be to decontaminate fast, neutralise if possible and get them back here quickly before they arrest as a result of absorption of the fluoride ions.'

One of the nurses came out of Resus armed to the teeth with the gel and plenty of calcium gluconate solution in a big green bag and handed it to Sarah.

'Right, let's hit the road,' Jack said, grabbing some of the gear and swinging the bag up over his shoulder. Matt grabbed another, Patrick took the last and Sarah followed with protective clothing and masks for them to put on as they arrived.

They went in Jack's car, a Mercedes estate with a magnetic green light and siren stuck on the roof and an illuminated sign in the back that said EMERGENCY DOCTOR ON CALL in bright green letters.

It was a hair-raising ride, and Sarah remembered someone telling her that Jack used to be a bit of a speed merchant in his younger days. It seemed he still hadn't forgotten how. She reminded herself of why they were doing it, and gritted her teeth.

Still, they arrived safely, to find a slather of ambulances, police cars and other vehicles clogging up the road. They managed to squeeze through towards the front with the aid of a policeman, but then a fireman stopped them going any further.

'Hydrofluoric acid,' he said tersely. 'You can't go in there, it melts plastic so your boots will dissolve. We'll bring the casualties to you.'

'Have you set up a flushing station anywhere?' Jack asked.

'Yes—by the engine. We're bringing the casualties out to there.'

They drove over to the fire engine, parked beside it and got out, quickly tugging on their protective gear. There wasn't time to worry about what they would see, which was just as well because the casualties, those that were still conscious, were screaming with pain.

Only four people had got any quantity of it on themselves, and one of them, the driver of the car that had hit the overturned lorry, was in a bad way. He'd staggered out of the car and slipped on the spill, then fallen into it.

The paramedic had been flushing him for five minutes already, but he was unconscious, and Jack's face was grim. 'Watch him, he's suffering from hypocalcaemia. Cover the skin with gel, give him IV and subcutaneous calcium and and get him back to the hospital stat. He's probably about to arrest.'

Matt and Sarah got the job of sorting him out while Jack and the others moved on. True to form, he arrested just as they were about to load him.

'More IV calcium,' Matt snapped.

Sarah was already handing it to him while a paramedic intubated the patient and started bagging him.

Matt thumped his chest, pumped the calcium into him as fast as he dared and tried again for a pulse.

'Anything?'

He shook his head. 'You'll have to take him as he is—keep him going all the way, they may be able to get him back at the hospital. Give him a hundred per cent oxygen and don't give up.'

The doors slammed behind the first ambulance, and it screeched off, siren wailing, as they turned to the next patient. She was the driver's wife and she'd tried to help him. She'd got it on her hands, knees and face, and was scrubbing at her eyes, making it worse. She'd been flushed but it didn't stop the pain, or the continuing burn.

Matt grabbed her wrists and held her hands down while Sarah smothered her face in gel, then they started on her hands and knees, before cutting away all her contaminated clothes and sealing them in a bag.

Once the woman was out of her clothes Sarah dressed the burns with gauze soaked in the calcium solution, Matt set up an IV, gave her morphine and a calcium injection and sent her off after her husband, with instructions for the ambulance crew to radio ahead about her eyes. Without specialist treatment she'd go blind, but if they hurried a simple corneal graft might save her sight. Her eyelids, though, might be a different story.

Patrick had finished the other two, the driver of the jackknifed lorry was taken to hospital, suffering from shock and a broken finger, and the onlookers started to drift away, strongly encouraged by the police.

Other people had needed treating—a fireman whose glove had slipped, a paramedic who'd had to kneel after his protective suit had been ripped by accident and a policeman who'd held someone's hand to comfort them and been contaminated.

However, all were now safely back at the hospital and a specialist clean-up team was decontaminating the area. It was getting dark by the time they got back to the hospital, to find that the driver of the car had died. Despite all their efforts they'd been unable to revive him because he'd had simply too much exposure for too long.

His wife was almost certainly blind, but the others were in the care of the plastic surgeons who were dealing with the aftermath of the burns.

Matt had acquired a tiny burn on his eyebrow, probably from a flailing patient, and Sarah washed it for him, covered it in gel and told him he'd need plastic surgery if his beauty wasn't to be permanently marred.

'I tell you what, it hurts like hell. What it must feel like to be covered in it I hate to think.'

'Want me to inject it with calcium gluconate?'

'If you must—and if you think it'll stop it hurting.'

'Poor baby.'

He rolled his eyes and settled back in the chair, leaning his head against the wall. He closed his eyes, and she rested her hand against his forehead to steady it while she infiltrated the area.

'Are you enjoying that?' he asked lazily.

'Oh, yeah. It's more fun than I've had in years.'

'I'm so glad.'

She removed the needle, bent it and disposed of it in the sharps bin, then stood, looking at him, with her hands on her hips. 'You can open your eyes now.'

His lids flicked up and those gorgeous grey-blue eyes locked with hers. 'Sadist,' he murmured.

She laughed. 'In your dreams, sunshine.'

He tsked. 'Damn. Thought it was my lucky night.'

They smiled, the tension and drama of the afternoon fading with the cock-eyed humour, and he stood up. 'Look at the time—I expect by now Ryan's picked Emily up.'

'Probably. Shall we get a take-away?'

'Good idea. I'm starving. Nothing like a bit of mayhem and blood-letting to sharpen the appetite.'

His timing was lousy. Jo Bailey, walking past on her way home after possibly her most difficult day so far, gave him a filthy look and ran out.

He shook his head. 'She's not going to make it. She's going to crack, without doubt, and this department is hardly the best place for her. I don't even think she's got a career in research, frankly.'

'She wants to be a GP.'

He laughed humourlessly. 'I don't think so. Oh, well, nothing we can do about it. Let's go.'

They picked up an Indian take-away from a Tandoori

restaurant on the way, and found Emily had been fed already with the O'Connor clan. Matt put her to bed, Sarah reheated the meal in the microwave and they settled down in front of the fire for a lazy supper on trays on their knees.

It was cosy and intimate and Sarah realised with surprise that it wouldn't have seemed at all odd to go up to bed together at the end of the evening. Were they really getting that close, or was it just her?

They made an exceptional team. They worked together almost in silence, each anticipating the other, and she knew she'd never worked this well with anyone before. They just seemed so in tune, so completely together in everything they did, and she wondered if that togetherness and anticipation would carry through to their love-making.

She knew it would. He'd know just how to touch her—

The thought stopped her in her tracks. Whatever was she doing, sitting here imagining them caught up in something so—so unplatonic? Colleague, she told herself for the millionth time. Just a colleague.

But he wasn't. Matt was a friend, and he was rapidly becoming more than a friend, at least to her.

She wondered if her feelings were reciprocated, but it was hardly something one asked, and he didn't seem to be about to volunteer the information. Indeed, she hadn't told him anything about her feelings, either, which was probably just as well, and if she had a shred of sense she'd keep it that way.

'How about an early night?' Matt murmured, cutting through her thoughts, and her eyes jerked up and met his before she could stop them. They were clear and calm and a little tired—and not the slightest bit suggestive of anything she'd been thinking about!

'Yes, it's been an awful day,' she said hastily. 'You go on up, I'll clear up in the kitchen. I'll see you in the morning.'

'I'll help you,' he offered, which wasn't at all what she wanted, but it was hard to get rid of him without arousing suspicion.

So they tidied the kitchen together, which took a very few minutes, and then headed up the stairs after Matt had checked the locks on the doors and turned out all the lights.

Just like a husband, she thought, and, saying goodnight hastily at the top of the stairs, she went into her room and closed the door with a decisive click.

She showered quickly, then she lay in bed and tried not to listen to him. It was hopeless. Modern houses like hers weren't designed to be soundproof. She heard his shoes fall one after the other, then the jingle of change and the clatter of his watch on the bedside table.

He went into the bathroom and showered, and she had to squeeze her eyes shut to try and block out the images.

Hopeless.

All she could see was his body, streaming with water, steam curling around him as he soaped and scrubbed those long, lean limbs. The water stopped and she imagined him stepping out of the shower and towelling himself roughly dry. He would be beaded with droplets, but he'd just swipe them with the towel—

Right on queue the bathroom door opened and she pictured him crossing the landing wrapped only in the towel, hair still damp and spiky, those droplets of water trickling down his neck and slithering down over that wonderful, well-muscled chest...

She was going nuts. She thumped the pillow, dragged the quilt up over her ears and resolutely ignored the noises from next door. Luckily the next night was her night for tin-shaking. Good. She'd be out all evening and wouldn't have to put up with this torture!

'Going out?'

Sarah smiled. 'Mmm—on the scrounge. I'm going to collect money.'

Matt gave her a quizzical look but said no more. Knowing what it would be like, she wrapped up warmly, went to the area organiser, picked up her collection box and went to the supermarket, where she stood in the foyer for four hours until they shut, and parted lots of people from their loose change.

It was quite a clever move, she decided, standing near the lottery machine. She played games with herself to see which way people would go. Some veered towards her when they saw her, foregoing the remote chance at however many million in favour of supporting the cot-death charity they could understand. Others bought a lottery ticket and couldn't meet her eye. Others bought a ticket and then gave her some money out of conscience. She was hardly ever right about who would do which.

Whatever the reason, though, at the end of the night she'd got a heavy collecting tin and a few more brownie points on her card.

She went home and found Matt in front of the television. 'Want a cup of tea?' she asked, poking her head round the door.

'Sounds good.'

She made it and went back in, kicking her shoes off and curling up in her chair.

'Get any money?'

'Mmm—lots. What are you watching?'

'A documentary. It's just started. It's about surrogacy.'

She froze. 'What?'

'It's an interview with a woman who's had three babies for other people. It's interesting.'

Sarah didn't find it interesting. She found it riveting, compelling, heart-rending—'interesting' didn't even begin to touch it.

At the end, when the woman talked about her babies and began to cry, Sarah got up and left the room.

She didn't need to see it.

She knew exactly how the woman felt.

She'd been there.

CHAPTER FIVE

'SARAH?'

She was standing at the kitchen sink with her back to Matt, and she felt his hands close gently over her shoulders.

'Talk to me.' His voice was soft and gravelly, coaxing.

She sat down at the table by the window and looked out into the darkness. She could just see the trees, swaying in the light wind. It was cold tonight. There'd probably be another frost—

'Sarah?'

His hand closed over hers, his thumb curving across her wrist, comforting silently.

'I had a friend,' she began. 'Her name was Helen. We were pregnant together, but when I had Toby she lost her baby in a traumatic delivery with disastrous consequences. They had to do a hysterectomy. It was awful. They were so close, and they were gutted. Brad was getting on—thirty-six then, pushing too old for adoption agencies to consider, and anyway he desperately wanted a child of his own.

'So did Helen, but her arms just ached to hold a baby, and sometimes she'd come and watch me with Toby and cry her eyes out. It was a sort of torture for her, but she couldn't seem to stay away. She needed a baby more than anyone I've ever met, and having babies was something I was good at.'

She paused, remembering, and then continued, 'I talked to Rob about it, and I don't really know where the idea came from—if it was him or me. I suspect it might have been him, because I probably wouldn't have suggested it in case he didn't like the idea. Anyway, we invited them round for a meal and discussed the idea of me carrying their baby for them. She still had ovaries, you see, so it would be really theirs.'

Her mouth curved in a smile. 'They jumped at it. They'd been wondering if they could ask me, but hadn't dared. I had James, whom I'd been pregnant with at the time we suggested it, and then once I'd recovered we all went together to a clinic in London where Helen's eggs were harvested.'

'How was Rob about all this?'

She smiled. 'Wonderful. He was a very good person, and if he could have done it himself I'm sure he would have done. He adored the boys, and he knew what Brad and Helen were missing.'

His thumb brushed her wrist idly. 'So what happened then?'

'The IVF failed. They gave it several goes, but the eggs died before they could be implanted, all but one, which didn't take. In the end they decided the only way would be if I was prepared to have Brad's baby by artificial insemination—which would mean it was my baby, too.'

'And didn't Rob mind?'

'No. Like I said, he would have done it himself. We all talked it over, but we were so far down the line by this time that it seemed the obvious thing to do, and not so very different from what we'd planned anyway. So, on the appointed day we went back to the clinic and with the help of a pipette and a technician, I conceived Brad's baby. She was born eight and a half months later, one week early, on the nineteenth of July.'

Sarah looked down at her hands, still held by his, and

he laid the other one over it as if he realised they were getting to the hard part. It was curiously comforting to feel the hard warmth of his fingers curled around hers.

She went on, 'I wasn't going to feed her at first, but it seemed wrong not to give her the colostrum. She needed it, and it was such a simple thing to do. It might have been easier if I hadn't done it.'

His hands squeezed gently, encouraging her.

'I fed her twice—at birth and again about three hours later—and then Helen and Brad took her away. They were overjoyed. They'd been there at the birth and I'll never forget their faces when she was born. They were so happy.'

There was a long, painful silence.

'And you?' Matt said softly. 'How were you?'

She gave a despairing little laugh. 'I was empty. I felt like Helen had when she'd lost her child. I didn't cry. Rob did, and I hugged him, but I just had this huge empty void inside and I couldn't cry. It wasn't as if she was dead, after all. She was alive, and loved, and with her father. I couldn't have chosen a better or more loving couple to be her parents, so there was really nothing to be sad about.'

'But still you missed her.'

'Oh, yes, every minute. Rob suggested we had another baby. I wasn't sure. It might have helped, I don't know. I never found out because he and the boys died five weeks later.' She gave a strained little laugh. 'Not a brilliant summer, really.'

His hands tightened. 'How did you cope?'

She shook her head. 'I didn't, not really. I had endless help at first—Cruse, the bereavement people, were wonderful, and so were the Samaritans when I was ready to end it. It was only the thought that she was still out there that kept me sane, that some day Helen and Brad might pop in and say, "Hey, look who's here!"'

'And did they?'

'No. No, of course not. We'd agreed that they wouldn't have any further contact with us. I felt it would be too difficult, and anyway Brad had a very unsettled job. He seemed to work all over the world, and it would have been impractical to try and keep up. Anyway, one day I decided I'd wallowed long enough, so I did some back-to-work retraining and returned to nursing. And here I am,' she said, smiling brightly, 'back in Suffolk near my parents, rattling round in a huge empty house and coming home alone—'

Her voice cracked, and Matt's hands tightened. She knew her smile must be strained, but Matt's was too. Tough guy that he was, with his gallows humour and flippant way of dealing with tragedy, for once he let her see the real man and his feelings.

His eyes were bright and he was visibly moved by her story. For a long time they said nothing, just sat there with their hands locked together so tightly their knuckles were white, and then she eased hers free and squeezed his fingers as she released them.

'Sorry. Enough of that. I don't very often talk about it, and I certainly don't make such a meal of it. It's just that film. I knew what she was going to say, and it brought it all crashing back. I'm all right, really.'

'You sure?'

She nodded. 'Yes, I'm sure. I think I might go up to bed now.'

She stood up and pressed a hand to his shoulder. 'Thanks for listening.'

'My pleasure,' he said, and his voice was rough. 'I'll lock up.'

'Thanks.'

She ran lightly up the stairs, intent on escape, but on the way she paused in Emily's doorway.

Her little one would be about the same age. Was she happy? Loved? Well?

Of course she was. How silly. And anyway, she wasn't her little one, she was Brad and Helen's. She didn't even know the child's name.

She went quietly into her bedroom and pulled out the photograph albums. Rob, and the boys, and then at the end the baby, tiny and furious, with a shock of black hair and skin like a little prune.

She smiled at the memory.

The last photo was of Brad and Helen, holding the baby and looking down at her with such wonder and joy that Sarah knew she was all right.

She sighed softly, closed the album and slid it back into the top of her wardrobe. Maybe one day she'd show Matt. Just for now, though, she was tired. She crawled into bed, put her head down and went straight to sleep...

Matt stayed at the table for an age, haunted by the memory of Sarah's face. She'd watched the documentary with such painful intensity that he could almost feel it coming off her in waves. He hadn't been sure that she'd talk to him, but she seemed to be able to unburden herself with him in a way he felt she didn't do very often.

He heaved a sigh. He'd wanted to get closer to her, and he'd certainly done that tonight. OK, she'd retreated to bed now, but not before she'd put another—very important—piece in the jigsaw that was Sarah Cooper.

He could have wept for her. It wouldn't have been hard—he could feel the lump in his throat even now—but he didn't. Instead, he cleared up the kitchen, tidied the sitting room and checked the doors, before turning out the lights and heading for the stairs.

Like an old married couple, he thought, and stifled a laugh of frustration. Perhaps not quite. If they were married he wouldn't be going to bed alone.

He checked Emily, tucking the quilt round her shoulders and dropping a feather-light kiss on her cheek. Bless her, she was infinitely precious. Of course, if he and Sarah were married Em would have a mother but, tempting as it sounded there were a lot of bridges to cross before they reached that point.

He wasn't sure if they ever would, but after tonight he felt they were that much closer. One thing was sure— whatever happened in the future, it would be governed by Emily and what was best for her. No matter what, the little girl, lying there with a battered teddy in her arms, definitely came first...

Neither of them said anything more about Sarah's baby, but knowing that she had no secrets from him any more made Sarah feel closer to him, as if they had a deeper understanding.

Which was daft, she thought, because he had hardly told her anything of his life in Canada. It didn't seem relevant, though, and it wasn't as if he was being secretive. He just didn't want to talk about his ex-wife, and that seemed quite reasonable to Sarah.

Workwise they continued to develop into a slick and polished team. When he wasn't around and she had to work with someone else, she often found it quite hard to anticipate what was needed.

'You asleep?' Patrick asked her one day.

'No—why?'

'I asked for sugar, blood, protein, bile and urobilinogen tests, and culture and microscopy at the lab, and you've included a pregancy test.'

Sarah blinked and looked at the forms. 'Yes.'

'Why?'

'She's in her mid-thirties—she could be pregnant.'

'Sarah, she's a *nun*.'

Matt, she realised, would have ordered the test anyway, just to be on the safe side. In the end Patrick did, too, but not without argument.

The initial results indicated a straightforward but massive urinary tract infection, explaining the severe abdominal and back pain and urinary retention. The patient was admitted overnight for supervision and further tests to find the cause of her problems, and Patrick teased Sarah about her suspicious mind.

'Pregnant nuns—whatever next?'

'I had a nun at my convent school who became pregnant,' said Kathleen Lawrence, Jack's Irish wife and ex-Sister of the A and E unit, 'so it's not so daft of her to check.'

'Did you have to choose today to bring the baby in?' Patrick asked drily. 'I need allies, not enemies.'

Kath laughed. 'Got to keep you in order, Patrick,' she said with a chuckle. The baby, two years old and a little tearaway like her father, ran giggling down the corridor and was carried back on his shoulders, shrieking and laughing and causing chaos.

'I think you'd better take this little monster home before she causes a disaster,' Jack said, swinging her down and dumping her into her mother's lap. 'I'll see you later.'

He kissed them both and wandered off, whistling, while Kath stood Colleen on her feet, grabbed her hand before she could run off again and waved goodbye to them all, before disappearing.

'She's gorgeous,' Sarah said wistfully.

Patrick gave her a searching look. 'How are you getting on with Matt?' he asked.

Sarah laughed uncomfortably. 'Was that remark connected?'

His shoulders moved almost imperceptibly. 'He's single, so are you, he's got a lovely daughter—you could do worse.'

It was too close to home—too close by far to the dreams she'd been nurturing the past few days and nights. 'Maybe he's not on the market, Patrick,' she said gently. 'And maybe I'm not, either.'

There was a rude snort by way of a reply, and they went back out to tackle the rest of the weekend rush. There was no time for any further conversation about personal matters, which suited Sarah down to the ground because Patrick had started to encroach on areas that were too sensitive, too new and hopeful and tentative to bear examination.

Still, there was a downside. Sarah had hoped for a quiet day, but it seemed she was doomed. It was a pity because it was the charity dinner that night and she would have liked a shred of energy left to cope with it.

Still, it couldn't be helped. At least she had tomorrow and Monday off. She threw herself back into the fray and tried to concentrate on working with Patrick, which was easy, really, because he was a very straightforward and methodical man.

They had the usual spate of abdomens and chests and heads and sore throats, in amongst the fractures and sports injuries which dominated Saturdays in the football and rugby season.

Unfit solicitors who played for the rugby club C team were a common sight, and this Saturday they had two—not surprisingly, because they'd had a head-on collision.

They came in together and sat making wisecracks through each other's consultations, both of them smothered in mud and hard to distinguish from one another.

One had a broken nose, the other a hairline fracture in his jaw, and Patrick sent them off, clutching head injury cards and follow-up appointments, with warnings to the jaw patient not to chew on the left-hand side and to come back immediately if it felt unstable.

Patrick watched them go and sighed. 'I don't think it's the first time that nose has been fractured,' he said drily.

'Probably won't be the last. Nasty game, rugby.'

Patrick grinned. 'I think it's the mentality of the players, not the game itself that's at fault. They're all ruddy nutters.'

She laughed. 'Muddy nutters, you mean. Look at the state of this place! Oh, well, at least they only mucked up one cubicle. I'll get the cleaning crew in to deal with it.'

She was about to call them when the phone rang. She went to find Patrick. 'As if we aren't busy enough, there's an elderly lady coming in with severe abdominal pain, vomiting and bloody diarrhoea. They picked her up in the shopping centre.'

'I hope you're going to do a pregnancy test on her—after all, it could be an ectopic—or maybe she's going in the *Guinness Book of Records*!'

'Pig!' She hit him, but not hard. She didn't want to injure him, he was too useful—and if he was out of action, she might have to work with the dreaded Jo Bailey.

The ambulance arrived a moment later and the woman was wheeled in, looking pale, shocked and very distressed.

'It's all right, my love, you're in safe hands,' Sarah assured her. 'Let's have a look at you and find out what's the matter. This is Dr Haddon, and I'm Sarah. What's your name, darling?'

'Dora,' she replied shakily, and started to cry. 'Ooh, it does hurt!' she moaned, and Patrick looked up at Sarah. His hands had been gently checking her out for the past few seconds, and he raised one eyebrow. His voice was low, too low for the patient to hear, but Sarah knew what he was going to say.

'Distension, tenderness, shock, no bowel sounds—I think she's got a mesenteric infarct. Let's have FBC, U and Es, blood sugar, cross-match four units and we'll get an IV up.'

'ECG?'

'Wouldn't hurt—and call the surgical team.'

Patrick found a vein and put a cannula in, then, while Sarah took the bloods and set up an infusion, Patrick explained to Dora what he thought the problem was.

'I think a piece of the membrane that supports your gut's got a little problem with its blood supply, and that's why you're having all this pain. Now, we want to do some tests and that's why we're taking the blood, and then we want to have a little look at what's going on with your ticker, just to make sure it's coping. OK?'

'Will I have to have an operation?' she asked anxiously.

'Possibly. We'll see. Is there anyone you'd like us to contact?'

'My daughter, please. I'd like her with me.'

'Of course you would.' Patrick turned to Sarah. 'Could you take the details and get someone onto it? I'll go and speak to the surgical reg.'

It was long past time for her to go before Sarah handed Dora over to the surgical team and left her. Her daughter had been held up, and she'd hung onto Sarah's hand so fiercely she hadn't had the heart to go.

As a result, she rushed in, shot into the shower and scrubbed the smell of the hospital from her skin, washed her hair and bundled it into a towel and went down to the kitchen in her robe, hair piled up in a turban, to find Matt and Emily in there, cooking.

'We've made supper,' Emily told her proudly. 'Look. I made some cakes for dessert, but Daddy says we can't have any yet until we've had our spaghetti.' She tipped her head on one side and regarded Sarah thoughtfully. 'Are you going to eat like that?'

Sarah realised with a sinking, horrible feeling that she hadn't told Matt she wouldn't be here. She'd meant to, but it had slipped her mind in the rush.

'Um—actually, I'm going out tonight,' she began, and Emily's face fell.

'But I can manage a little because I won't have supper until very, very late and I'll be starving by then,' she lied. In fact, the meal was scheduled for eight-thirty, and she was going to be pushing it to get there on time as it was, unless she put her nail varnish on now—

'Tell you what, you dish up and I'll go and get a bit more ready,' she told them, and ran upstairs, without looking at Matt.

She slapped her nail varnish on faster than she'd ever done it, dried it with the hairdryer and then turned her attention to her hair. She'd meant to curl it and put it up in a sort of frothy style, but it probably wouldn't have worked and, anyway, she didn't have time, so she brushed it out straight, ran the dryer over it a few times and shot downstairs just as Matt came out of the kitchen.

'I'm really, really sorry,' she muttered, meeting his eyes for the first time. Blast. They were disappointed. In her, or in her absence? Both, probably. Oh, well, it was his fault. He had her so distracted she didn't know what she was doing.

The meal was passable, but she really didn't need to

eat so much. The small-talk, on the other had, was fraught with difficult silences.

'So, is this a last-minute invitation?' Matt said casually during one of them.

'Last-minute? Oh—no, I just forgot to mention it.'

'He must be riveting.'

She thought of dear old George who'd helped her organise the dinner and suppressed a giggle. 'He is. Emily, this bun is delicious. Well done.'

'We made a dreadful mess,' she confessed. Sarah glanced over her shoulder and winced.

'Tell you what, as my contribution to the meal, why don't you let me clear up?'

'And salve your conscience? No way,' Matt muttered under his breath.

'Oh, come on,' she said, trying to placate him. 'I didn't know you were planning anything. You should have told me.'

'Some surprise it would have been.'

She dropped her napkin on the table and stood up. 'Look, I'm sorry. I have to go now. Emily, thank you, darling.'

She bent and kissed the little rosy cheek, dusted with flour and icing sugar, and fled upstairs to put on her make-up and change. It took ten minutes, a record, and yet still about five minutes too long.

She ran downstairs, still wrestling with a slingback strap on her evening sandals, and went smack into Matt's chest.

His hands steadied her, and she straightened to see the look of disapproval replaced by admiration in his eyes as they skimmed over her bare shoulders.

'You look lovely,' he said softly. 'Enjoy yourself, you deserve to. I'm sorry I was a grouch.'

'And I'm sorry I spoiled your surprise.'

He held her coat for her, tucking it up under her chin with clucking noises about getting chilled, and then without warning he bent forward and dropped a kiss on her cheek. 'Off you go, Cinderella. Your carriage just pulled up outside.'

He opened the front door and stood there, and Sarah wondered if he was trying to see the driver—not that it would help him. It was a mini-cab driver, picking George up on the way as well and taking them both to the hotel.

She wondered why she hadn't told Matt that it was a charity dinner that she was helping with, but decided it didn't matter. It might help to diffuse the heat that was beginning to simmer between them.

She lifted her hand and laid it over her cheek. She could still feel the warm imprint of his lips…

The kitchen was immaculate when she got back at two the next morning. To her surprise, Matt was still in the sitting room, stretched out full length on the sofa, watching some mindless cops-and-robbers film through his eyelids. She flicked off the television and he struggled up. 'Wha—?' he muttered, and she smiled and pushed him down again, perching on the sofa so that her hip nudged his.

'Waiting up for me?' she asked with gentle reproach.

He grinned sheepishly. 'Not really. I was watching something on organ transplantation, but I was too comfortable to move when it ended.'

'So you stayed there. Seems logical. I've put the kettle on—fancy a cup of tea?'

'Sounds good,' he mumbled, scrubbing his hands over his face. 'Ah, I feel like I'm on call.' He yawned hugely, showing off even white teeth.

'You've had your tonsils out.'

He laughed and shut his mouth. 'You spotted.'

'Difficult not to. I saw your gastric ulcer as well.'

'Damn, I was hoping to keep that one a secret.'

His grin teased at her nerves, and she was suddenly conscious of the warmth and hardness of his hip against hers. She stood up and went out to the kitchen to make the tea, and he followed her.

'So, how was your dinner date?'

'Fine. Excellent. Made lots of money.'

He did a mild double-take, and she giggled.

'It was a charity do,' she told him, putting him out of his misery. 'SIDS—sudden infant death syndrome. I support it. In fact, I helped to organise the dinner tonight.'

'Didn't your date mind?'

'He's sixty-eight, he has gout and, no, he didn't mind—he helped too. His name's George and he's wonderful and I love him to bits.'

'But he's not on your list.'

Her brows pleated together. 'My list?'

'Of possibles for an affair.'

'I don't have a list,' she told him firmly, but she couldn't meet his eyes. She did have a list, in fact—a very short list.

Extremely short.

He didn't need to know that, though, and particularly not tonight when it was this late, she was shattered and he was eyeing her bare shoulders as if he'd like to bite them.

'About this mother of yours who's a vampire,' she murmured, and his eyes flicked guiltily up to hers.

'What?'

'Stop staring at my neck as if you'd like to sink your teeth into it.'

He chuckled, colouring slightly. 'Sorry. It just looks—
you look—very lovely tonight.'

She felt a warm glow of pleasure touch her skin.
'Thank you.'

There was a sudden, electric silence. She cleared her
throat and broke it. 'Um—I think I'll turn in. You
shouldn't have done the kitchen, by the way. I said I'd
do it.'

'So I have to do it when you mess it up?' He laughed.
'No way. You'll do some amazing fancy thing that uses
every pan in the place.'

'Of course. I have to impress you—but it won't be a
surprise. I shall make quite sure you're here, and hungry.'

'Oh, I will be.'

They suddenly weren't talking about food any more,
and the electric silence was back.

'Um—goodnight, Matt. Thanks for waiting up.'

She turned on her heel and fled, leaving him standing
at the bottom of the stairs gazing up at her. She didn't
look back. She daren't. For two pins she would have
invited him into her room to finish what that look had
started.

Sunday was a gorgeous day. It began with a frost—and
Emily, bouncing onto the middle of her bed, right on
her stomach, and grinning into her face.

'I've got a wobbly tooth,' she announced, and stuck
her finger in her mouth and wiggled it.

'So you have.' Sarah pushed the hair out of her eyes,
struggled up the bed and lay propped on the pillows,
fighting sleep, while Emily chattered about teeth and
cookies and cinnamon rolls and Daddy, until her nose
finally identified the gorgeous smell drifting up the
stairs.

'Is he cooking?'

Emily nodded hugely. 'Uh-huh. Breakfast in bed. He told me to come and wake you up gently.'

'Oh. Right.' She squashed the smile. Gently? There was no way youngsters woke you up gently.

Except Toby, when she'd come home from the hospital, feeling drained, and he'd crept into her room and kissed her softly until her eyes had opened...

'Can I get into bed with you? It's chilly out here. My feet are freezing. Feel...'

And she stuck her icy feet on Sarah's arm.

Sarah gave a little shriek and let the child snuggle in beside her. Her arm seemed to find a natural resting place around Emily, and the little girl wriggled closer, stuck her finger in her mouth and wiggled her tooth some more.

'It feels funny,' she told Sarah.

'I know. I can remember when I had wobbly teeth.'

Emily took her finger out of her mouth and lay still for a minute. 'Daddy says we're going for a walk today if you want to come too. He doesn't know where to go, but he says you might. Will you come?'

And get even more attached to you?

'Maybe. Depends what time.'

'We'll ask Daddy.'

She settled down again, and a few moments later Matt appeared in the doorway, tray in hand, and found them snuggled together.

'Looks kinda cosy,' he murmured.

Sarah smiled. 'Her feet were like ice. Doesn't she have any slippers?'

'Oh, yes, and slipper socks. She just doesn't bother. She usually warms them on me.'

They shared a smile of commiseration, interrupted by Emily. 'Sarah's nicer to cuddle than you—she's all soft.

Why don't you get in and cuddle up too, like a real family?'

Sarah choked down a laugh at the discomfiture on Matt's face.

'Ah, I don't think so, honey. Um—why don't you—er—move over a little so you've got room for your plate and then I can give Sarah her cup of tea?'

'There's lots of room in here for you, look!' Emily persisted, throwing back the quilt and showing him the spare acres of mattress on her side. 'Or I can move over if you want to sit next to Sarah, but I'd rather be in the middle.'

'Um—I'll just stay here, sweetheart, on the side. I have to go down and check the oven in a minute.'

'Oh.' She subsided, crestfallen for a brief second, then squirmed up the bed, took her plate and sank her teeth into a bun. 'My tooth's wobbling,' she told them—at least, that was what it might have been.

'Don't talk with your mouth full—where are you going now?'

'To get my teddy. He's hungry.'

She ran out of the room and Matt passed Sarah a cup of tea, Their eyes met ruefully.

'I'm sorry,' he murmured.

She chuckled. 'Don't be, she's gorgeous.'

'I'm very tempted,' he confessed with an intimate smile. 'It looks really cosy in there.'

Sarah felt her skin warm, and she was relieved when Emily came back and broke the tension sizzling between them. The rest of their breakfast passed without incident, and when they were all ready they set off in Matt's car for the park.

They took some stale bread and the remains of the cinnamon rolls and fed the ducks. Then they found the playground, and after Emily had finally exhausted the possibilities of all the equipment they wandered around the arboretum at the side, up and down the wooded tracks under the strangely named trees.

They went back the long way round, and Sarah showed them a little of the Suffolk countryside before they went home for lunch.

'Right, isn't it time we did something in your garden? I've been here three weeks now and we still haven't tackled it.'

'Is it really that long?'

'Sure is.'

In a way it felt longer. Sarah was getting terribly used to having them there, but it wouldn't last for ever. It was nearly February already, and they left at the end of March. Nine more weeks.

Not nearly long enough—but, then, she was beginning to think that a lifetime with Matt and Emily wouldn't be long enough. Nine weeks didn't even scratch the surface.

CHAPTER SIX

SARAH spent Monday in the garden as well, finishing the tidy-up she and Matt had started the day before. It was only a reasonably small garden, quite quick to do once she got out there and confronted it, but it had always been Rob who'd done the garden in Gloucestershire and she'd never really been interested.

Now, though, she was happy to potter among the images of Matt and Emily, and after school on Monday she picked Emily, Gus and Evie up from school and brought them all back for tea.

Ginny came round at six to remove her two, and they had a cup of tea in the kitchen while the children tidied up the games they'd got out.

'So, how's it going with Matt?' Ginny asked, direct as ever.

'Oh—all right. He's a very civilised house-guest.'

'I didn't ask if he washes up,' Ginny teased.

'I know—and I'm ignoring you.'

'He's a nice guy.'

'I know he is.'

'And he's single.'

'I know he is.'

'And Emily could do with a mum.'

Sarah stood up and went to the sink, washing her cup distractedly. 'I don't think it's fair to bring Emily into this. If anything happens between us, it needs to be because it's right for us, and nothing to do with Emily. She's really not part of the equation.'

'I'm glad we agree on that.'

She whirled to see Matt, standing in the doorway, regarding her steadily. 'Um—hi.'

'I'll go,' Ginny said, leaping to her feet and diving past Matt. 'Kids, come on, time to go. Daddy will be home soon.'

'Oh, do we have to? We're playing with Emily—'

'Come on.'

Matt closed the door. 'What was that all about?'

She shrugged. 'Ginny was matchmaking. She does it all the time. She thinks I need a man.'

'And do you?'

Yes—you, she could have told him, but she didn't. 'I've survived for five years without.'

'Is it what you want?'

'Is there a point to this?'

'Sarah, when's Daddy—? Oh, you're here! Hiya!'

He squatted and hugged her. 'Hi, sprout. Had a good day?'

'Yup—and you?'

'OK. Not too bad. Had your supper?'

She nodded. 'With Gus and Evie. We had fish fingers and beans and chips.'

'Yuck.'

'It was great! You ought to try it.'

He laughed and straightened. 'No, thank you. I prefer something a little more sophisticated.'

Sarah let her breath ease out on a sigh. Had he let the subject go? Knowing Matt, probably not—or not for long. She busied herself at the sink, scrubbing potatoes, topping and tailing beans and cleaning a couple of trout she'd bought in the fishmonger's at lunchtime.

'Hey, that looks good.'

'Do you like trout?'

'I love all fish—just so long as it doesn't have fingers. Am I included in the dinner invitation?'

'That depends on how many silly questions you're going to ask,' she threatened with a laugh.

'I'll behave.'

'Then, yes, you are included. Go and change—you smell of antiseptic scrub.'

'Wow, a potent aphrodisiac.'

'Not!'

He grinned and went out, and she could hear him whistling as he moved around upstairs. She put the trout under the grill, put the beans on to boil, checked the jacket potatoes and ran upstairs to change out of her gardening clothes.

Bad move. He was coming out of the shower dressed in soft jersey boxer shorts, and her heart slammed up against her ribs.

'Come to get me?' he asked, totally unselfconscious, and she shook her head. No way was she following that one up!

'Ten minutes,' she said, and shot into her room, closed the door and leaned against it with a sigh. Darn the man, he was just too sexy for words!

She'd been right in her fantasies—he didn't dry himself properly. There'd been beads of moisture clinging to the light dusting of hair on his chest, and as she'd stood there transfixed, like a rabbit in headlights, it had dribbled down his chest and slid into the waistband of those sinfully sexy boxers.

It played hell with the concentration. She changed quickly, ran downstairs and rescued the trout from under the grill in the nick of time.

Sarah was glad she'd spent two days relaxing and pottering in the garden, because that week all hell broke loose at work.

The weather was bad again, another cold snap with

snow this time, and they were deluged with Colles' fractures and hips in the elderly. At one point there were thirty-six patients waiting for new hip-replacement surgery, on top of the elective list, and all elective surgery was cancelled until the backlog was dealt with.

The orthopaedic teams were rushed off their feet, and Ryan disappeared to help for a day on Thursday to try and reduce the waiting time.

It didn't help the A and E department at all because the stream of patients coming in didn't diminish just because Ryan wasn't there. In the end they called him back in desperation because a nasty RTA came in with several casualties and all skilled medical personnel were needed to deal with it.

Sarah and Matt were together, as usual, and Jo Bailey was sent to deal with the usual run of waiting-room patients that they hoped would be within her capabilities. She was shaping up better, in fairness, but she still found the really grisly trauma difficult, and she'd never got the hang of their repartee. Sarah was glad she wasn't around because the cases were all grim and she would have freaked.

They worked for the most part in silence, with occasional comment from someone about blood pressure or sinus rhythm, and then they would pause and do whatever was necessary to preserve life until the patient was stabilised again and they could continue the clean-up and evaluation of other less immediately life-threatening injuries.

Their patient had arrested three times before they finally admitted defeat, and that was only because a living but fragile patient was on the way in from the RTA on the brink of disaster and needed help fast.

'We have to prioritise,' Matt said heavily. 'This one's

a waste of time but the woman might not be. We have to do what we can, but we aren't God.'

Sarah sighed and stood back, stripping off her gloves and gown. 'OK, let's take a look at her.'

She washed, changed into fresh gown and gloves and they started again the moment she arrived.

Tom Hallam, the paramedic who'd been bitten by the dog, brought her in and reeled off the treatment so far.

'She was one of the drivers—steering wheel injury, deformed and twisted to the right, crush injuries to the legs, conscious when we got there but she's been in and out, mainly out. Teeth seem broken and loosened—we sucked out the broken bits. She's got tachycardia and she's in shock, and she was trapped for over half an hour. She's had two units of Haemaccel.'

'Thanks. OK, let's intubate her. Watch that neck—we need the mobile X-ray in here now. I want cervical spine, CXR—'

'She's got a flail, I reckon.'

Matt glanced down at her chest which another nurse was rapidly revealing with the scissors. 'Yup. Right, immobilise that with a hard pillow to stop the lungs bruising.' He slid the cuffed tube home, inflated the little cuff that sealed the airway and held it in place, and Sarah connected it up to pure oxygen.

'Right, let's get some leads on her. How's her pressure?'

'Lousy—sixty over forty.'

'Too low. Her neck veins are distended as well. Is that trachea in the midline?' he murmured, feeling for himself. 'Damn, she's got cardiac tamponade. Nothing's ever easy, is it?'

Sarah handed him a 50 ml syringe attached to a long cardiac needle, without waiting for a request, and as soon as she'd lifted the backrest and patient to about thirty degrees he felt beside the tip of the sternum, moved slightly to the left, entered the chest wall horizontally and then tipped the needle back so it pointed upwards towards the heart.

'Get a V-lead on the needle so I can see if I hit the heart,' Matt ordered, but Sarah was already there, and she continued placing the other leads at lightning speed so he could see exactly what the heart was doing.

'I think I felt it pop,' he murmured, drawing back on the syringe, and Sarah watched in satisfaction as it filled with the blood that had been surrounding the heart inside its membrane, putting pressure on it and preventing it from working.

She put a clamp against the skin so that movements of the patient's chest wouldn't advance the needle any further, and then watched the monitor.

Immediately the cardiac output and blood pressure picked up, and Matt withdrew the needle once the blood stopped flowing. 'Right, let's have her flat again and have a look at the rest of her abdomen and legs. I reckon she might have a ruptured bowel as well.'

He glanced over at Ryan. 'How are you doing?'

'Oh, you know. Ruptured diaphragm, maybe bowel— he's just about stable now. I reckon I'm going to send him up to Theatre. They're standing by. I think Oliver's about—want him to look at yours?'

'Could do. Looks pretty messy.'

'What happened to the other one?'

Matt ran his finger across his throat, and Ryan nodded.

'You win some, you lose some. We aren't God.'

They certainly weren't. They lost two out of six of the casualties that were brought in from the accident, and by the time they sat down in a quiet moment it was six o'clock. Considering the RTA had happened before lunch, that was pretty lousy going.

'Don't you just hate people?' Matt said lazily, sprawl-ing in the staffroom and peering into a cup of tepid cof-fee. 'It was a nice day today until they decided to kill themselves.'

'Highly inconsiderate,' Ryan agreed from the depths of his chair.

Jack had gone home, Sarah was technically off duty and the only other person in the staffroom was Jo Bailey.

She was maintaining a chilly silence, ignoring them with studied emphasis, and Matt rolled his head towards her. 'Cheer up, Jo, it may never happen,' he said with a grin.

'It happens every day in here,' she said flatly.

'Getting to you?'

'Of course—and if it doesn't, you lot do.' She put her cup down with a clatter. 'Did it occur to you that those people that died may not have wanted to? Maybe they had husbands and wives and children and parents—lov-ers, friends—but they were just a nuisance to you, in-terfering with your *nice day*! Just tell me something— why can't you care? What's wrong with having feelings?' she asked desperately.

Matt sat forward. 'Nothing—except feelings get hurt.'

'Maybe they *need* to get hurt. Maybe you're all out of touch with what's going on out there.'

'I don't think so,' Ryan said drily from the corner. 'I think we're all too well aware of just how much is at stake when we give up on someone. That's why, very often, we go on too long.'

'How can you go on too long?'

'When people don't want to be saved—when what we're saving them for isn't worth having. It's a grim world down here, Jo. Maybe you'd be better off in some nice, safe, unthreatening branch of the profession.'

'Like pathology, where I can't do any harm?' she suggested bitterly. 'I *want* to be a doctor.'

'So stick with it,' Matt drawled, sliding down the chair again, 'but for God's sake leave us alone while you do it, and let us deal with it in our own way.'

One of the nurses stuck her head round the door. 'Dr Bailey, you're needed out the front.'

She stood up tiredly and trailed out, and Sarah, watching her go, shook her head.

'I'm worried about her.'

'She'll survive.'

'I think there's something else wrong.'

'So talk to her. Invite her round for a meal at the weekend and chat about it.'

Sarah nodded. 'I might do that. Right, I'm going home. Are you two coming, or are you staying here for the night?'

'Yeah, right.' Matt laughed, and uncoiled himself from the chair. 'Take me home, country roads. I'm bushed.'

'Shall I drop Emily in to you on the way past?' Ryan offered.

'Would you? That way I can go and crawl into a nice, hot bath with a cup of tea or preferably something stronger, and forget today ever happened.'

Ryan laughed. 'Sounds good to me. See you later.'

They left the hospital, went back and dedicated the evening to relaxing. Emily was chirpy and delicious, and while Matt soaked in the bath she snuggled up next to Sarah with her reading book to do her homework, in between chattering about her friends and telling Sarah about the nest some birds were building.

'Mrs Bright says it's too early and the chicks will die—Sarah, can I bring them home here to keep warm?'

She hugged her, a lump in her throat. 'Sweetheart, that

won't work. They need their mother. You can't separate them, it wouldn't be fair. They've got more chance with her than without her.'

'But I could bring her too.'

Sarah patiently explained about baby birds and spring and how the birds wouldn't lay their eggs yet because it was too cold, and that even if they did they could always lay more later in the year.

Reassured, Emily settled down again and finished her reading, then Matt appeared dressed in ancient and obviously favourite jeans, a tired sweatshirt and socks.

'Better?'

'Heaps. Why don't you go and have a long, hot soak?'

She shook her head. Just the thought of lying in a bath he'd recently occupied made her nerve-endings tingle. Instead, she showered, threw together some supper for them all and they all had an early night.

It was just as well because the following morning was horrendous, and it started about as badly as it could.

They had a call from the doctors' residence to say someone had been found in a bath with slashed wrists and query overdose. Matt and Sarah ran through the hospital to the accommodation wing and were directed to the bathroom where the action all seemed to be happening.

'Can we get through, please?' Matt called, and all the people that were trying to help got out of the way, all giving their ten penn'orth. As the crowd parted they got their first look at the person.

'Oh, Lord, it's Jo,' Sarah whispered. 'I knew there was something wrong.'

'Damn. Right, let's get her out of the bath—keep her arms up and put pressure over those wrists. Has anybody got any towels we can wrap her in?'

Someone appeared with a hospital blanket, and they laid Jo on the floor on it, covered her with a towel for modesty and warmth and tried in vain to get a pulse.

'I've got one—very thin and fast. She's very shocked. She needs blood—she needs to be in A and E.'

'There's a trolley coming,' someone called.

They lifted her onto the trolley, ran back to A and E and took her straight into Resus. 'Blood for cross-match, but we'll start her on O neg. I'll get a line in—someone hold that pressure on her wrists.' Matt struggled to find the vein inside her elbow, but it collapsed just as he was almost there. 'Damn it, Jo, come on, don't do this. I'm not going to let you go.' He got it in the second time, opened the line and started the blood transfusion.

'I don't know if this is relevant,' someone said. They'd been followed back to A and E by one of the people who'd found her, and she was clutching a packet. 'Could she have taken these?'

Matt took the packet. 'Damn. Aspirin. Right, let's pump her out just in case. Keep up the pressure on those wrists, for God's sake. We're only just holding her as it is.'

They passed a lavage tube, washed out the remains of several pills and some 'coffee-grounds', partially digested blood from the irritated stomach wall.

'Silly girl,' Matt muttered. 'What a waste.'

'I've seen worse,' Sarah said, flushing and emptying over and over to get out every last bit. 'I think that's all. Charcoal?'

'Yes, fifty grams in a slurry down the tube. It's better than making her drink it when she comes to.'

Sarah poured the charcoal mixture in to absorb any last remaining aspirin, and then withdrew the tube.

Jo gagged, and Matt bent over her.

'Jo? Jo, you're in A and E. It's Matt—can you talk to me?'

Her eyes flickered open and she moaned softly. 'Let me go,' she pleaded.

'No way. Sorry, lady, you're a keeper. Jo, what have you taken?'

'Aspirin,' she whispered. She tried to reach for him but her arms were being held until he could get to them with sutures. 'Matt—is the baby OK?'

'Baby?'

'I'm pregnant.'

He swore, softly, under his breath, and Sarah moved to Jo's side and smoothed back the hair from her face. 'The baby seems fine at the moment. Let's worry about you first.'

'She'll need a catheter for forced diuresis to flush her system. Let's sort these wrists out and get some more blood into her before we do that, OK?'

'He wanted me to get rid of it. He said he didn't want it, or me—and you don't want me either, any of you...'

She started to cry, great heaving sobs that tore them all apart. 'Oh, Jo, that's not true,' Sarah told her gently, gathering her into her arms. While Matt stitched, grim-lipped and silent, and someone else squeezed blood into her, Sarah held her and rocked her gently and murmured soothingly until she relaxed and lay still.

'Matt, it's not your fault,' Sarah murmured to him as he tied the last suture.

'I shouldn't have told her to leave us alone.'

'Blood pressure's better,' someone said. 'Ninety over fifty.'

Sarah lifted her head and met Matt's eyes. 'I'll do the catheter. You go and have a cuppa—and make us one. I expect Jo might like something in a minute.'

It only took moments to put the urinary catheter in,

and Jo didn't say a word all the way through apart from asking Sarah to check that she wasn't bleeding.

'No. Looks fine. How far along are you?'

'Ten weeks.'

'Only thirty to go, then.'

Sarah's smile didn't get a reply. With a sigh she taped the catheter to Jo's leg, covered her up again and propped up her top end. 'How many aspirin did you take?'

She shrugged. 'The packet? There were about twenty-two—I'd just started them.'

'How did you take soluble aspirin dry?' Sarah asked, amazed.

Jo laughed wanly. 'With difficulty. They taste vile.'

'I know. I had to chew a couple once. I was nearly sick.' Sarah sat down beside her and took her bandaged hand. 'Why did you do it, Jo?'

'To kill myself?'

Her smile was weak and tearful, and made Sarah want to howl.

'Is it so bad?'

The smile faded, overtaken by the tears. 'He told me to get rid of it. I couldn't bear to—I thought this would be the easiest way, if I really had to.'

'You don't have to,' Sarah assured her vigorously. 'Lots of single women have babies these days.'

'Not single women doctors of twenty-six with eighty-hour weeks.'

'You could always take a break and come back later to finish your training.'

'If I wanted to. I'm not sure I do. I'm not sure I can hack it, all the blood and violence and horror.'

Sarah dropped her eyes. 'Look, Jo, I'm sorry we upset you with our jokes. They don't mean anything.'

'I know. I do understand. It's just that I've been under

so much pressure recently that I can't cope with it, and all of you playing the fool in the midst of such trauma was a bit difficult to take on top of everything else. It's not your fault.'

'But Matt feels it is. Last night he told you to go and sort yourself out somewhere else. It wasn't very supportive, and the rest of us were no better.'

Jo shrugged. 'He was shattered. He'd had a hell of a day, and so had the rest of you. I'd been lucky with all the scraped knees and broken wrists and so on. He was only telling me to get off his back, and I deserved it.'

Sarah squeezed her hand. 'Whatever. How are you feeling now?'

'Pretty gross. My stomach aches.'

'It will. That's the gastritis. I think you'd better have some tablets for that if you feel you can take them. I'll go and find Matt.'

'Matt's here. What did you need?'

'Antacids and cimetidine or something like that.'

'Done. It's here, with a cup of weak, tepid tea with lots of milk.'

'Yuck.'

He gave a crooked smile and set the tray down. 'I'm sorry, Jo—about all sorts of things. We've given you a hard time—'

'No. Please, this was nothing to do with you. I'm really grateful to you. I didn't really want to...die...'

The tears started again in earnest, and Sarah hugged her and stroked her hair while Matt held her hand and made soothing noises in the background.

Into this touching little scene strode Jack Lawrence, his eyes wide with worry. 'I just got here—what's going on?'

'Jo's been a bit silly,' Sarah said softly.

'So I gather. Mind if I have a chat with her?'

They left Jo with him and went into the staffroom for a cup of tea. Sarah was fine until Matt put his hand on her shoulder and said, 'OK?'

'Not really,' she mumbled, and before she could stop herself the tears welled over and tracked down her cheeks.

'Ah, hell, sweetheart,' Matt murmured, and pulled her gently into his arms. 'Silly girl.'

'She's pregnant and he doesn't want to know,' she snuffled into his shirt.

'I know.' His arms tightened. 'She'll be all right. She needs to get away for a while and think herself straight.'

'If she's got anywhere to go.'

'I feel a spare room coming on,' Matt teased.

'Well, I have got one. I could offer. She might not want to come to me.'

'Just give her the option. She more than likely won't take you up on it.'

Jack came in then. 'Silly kid. She's going up to the ward for the night, and then in the morning her mother will come and take her home and look after her. And lay off the sick jokes for a day or two, eh? We've all been hard on her.'

He went out again, and Matt and Sarah shrugged at each other. 'Oh, well, at least she won't need your spare room.'

Sarah smiled wanly. 'No. Oh, well, perhaps it's for the best. It could get a bit crowded with all of us there.'

Jo was transferred, and after a while they were all back to normal. Up to their eyes, in fact, as usual.

It was nearly six when Matt got home. Sarah had knocked off at five, on time for once, and picked Emily up on the way home. They made supper together, a sort of bolognese sauce with macaroni cheese on top that

Sarah called cheat lasagne, and it was almost ready when Matt arrived back.

'Smells good,' he said, smiling at them round the kitchen door. 'OK if I shower?'

'Be my guest. I'm going to have a long, hot bath later.'

They laid the table ready, and then went into the sitting room to watch a cartoon while Matt splashed about overhead. Funny, she was getting used to it now, and it seemed really quite right to have him here, pottering about doing all the intimate and personal things people did in their own homes.

She never felt crowded by him—in fact, quite often she felt lonely because they weren't as close as she would have liked.

He appeared in his comfy jeans again, and they ate the cheat lasagne and finished up with ice cream and tinned fruit. Then he went and put Emily to bed while Sarah wallowed in the bath.

She had to go into the main bathroom because there was only a shower in her *en suite* bathroom, and as she settled down in the piping hot water she could almost feel him there with her.

How did he fit? she wondered. He was much too big to fold himself up into this little tub, surely? His knees must stick out in all directions, and how did his shoulders fit?

It didn't do her any good at all, lying there thinking those sorts of thoughts, and in the end she got out, scrubbed herself roughly dry with a towel, wrapped it round her, wound another one round her head and opened the door.

Matt was standing there on the landing, just on his way out of Emily's room.

'She's out like a light—end of a long week.'

'Tell me about it.'

His eyes dropped to her shoulders and then flicked back up to her face. 'Get something warmer on and come down and relax. I've opened a bottle of wine to breathe.'

'Sounds lovely. Give me five minutes.'

'Two.'

So she put on her nightshirt with the crocodile on the front that said, MORNING, SEXY, pulled her old towelling robe over the top, picked up some slipper socks and went downstairs.

'Dressed to kill, you notice,' she said with a laugh as she went into the sitting room.

He smiled, a slow, lazy, thoughtful smile, and handed her a glass of wine.

'Cheers,' he murmured.

'Cheers.'

He sat on the sofa and patted the seat beside him. 'Come and join me.'

She laughed. 'Looking like this?'

'You look fine.'

'You need your eyes tested.'

'I don't think so.'

'I know so.'

'Just come here, woman, and stop arguing.'

She smiled and sat down sideways-on at the other end of the sofa, tucking her toes under the hard warmth of his thigh. 'Masterful, eh?'

He laughed. 'Is that the answer? Is that what I've been doing wrong all these years?' His hand came down to rest over her ankles, and she found her answer flew out of the window.

She tucked her nose into her glass of wine until she'd recovered her equilibrium, and watched him over the rim. He was a sight for sore eyes, she thought lazily, settling back further into the corner. He had his eyes closed, his head rested back against the cushions, and she watched the steady rise and fall of his chest and thought how right he looked there at the other end of her sofa.

'I wonder how Jo is?' he murmured.

'She's in good hands. I popped in to see her on the way out, and she was calmer. She's going to keep the baby, and she's going to think about her career. She might carry on and take maternity leave, or she might just give up and concentrate on being a mother, but her own mother seems to be being very supportive, which is wonderful.'

'She needs that. I still feel bad.'

'Perhaps it's a lesson learned, but I had a feeling something else was wrong with her. Anyway, I think she'll be OK.'

'Mmm.'

He settled further into his corner, and Sarah thought again how right he looked there. Right, and extremely long.

'How on earth do you fit in the bath?' she asked idly.

He chuckled. 'You'll have to come and see next time. It's quite an art.'

'I think I'll pass on that,' she said with a laugh. 'I doubt if I'd get through the door with you in there.'

'It might be quite fun, playing sardines,' he murmured, and their eyes locked. Her breath jammed in her throat, and reaching out one of those long arms he extracted her glass from her nerveless fingers, put both glasses down and stood up.

'You know I'm going to kiss you, don't you?' he warned softly, drawing her to her feet. 'If you don't want this, stop me now.'

Stop him? She couldn't have stopped him if her life

had depended on it. Instead, she lifted her face to his, closed her eyes and waited.

'Uh-uh. Open your eyes. You have gorgeous eyes. I want to see them go all misty when I kiss you.'

She could feel them go all misty now, and he was only talking about it! Her ribs were being beaten to death by her heart, her mouth felt suddenly dry and she thought she was going to faint. His hands tightened on hers and she watched, spellbound, as his head came down and his eyes locked with hers, smouldering with anticipation and desire.

His lips brushed hers softly, side to side, teasingly, then she felt the satin sweep of his tongue along the seam of her lips. They parted a fraction and he increased the pressure slightly, drawing a tiny moan from her throat.

'I've wanted to do this for so long,' he murmured against her lips, and then his mouth closed over hers and she whimpered and leaned into him. She needed to feel him, needed his body hard against hers, but he stood just out of reach, only their mouths and hands making contact.

It was the sweetest torture. She hadn't realised her mouth was so sensitive, but every touch of his tongue, every shift of his lips, drove her even higher. Their hands were locked together, only the firm grip of his preventing her from falling. She could feel her legs trembling, until finally they buckled and he was forced to hold her in his arms or drop her.

The shock of that first contact was electric. Heat poured off him, burning her, driving her crazy with a need that had lain dormant for so many years she could hardly remember it.

She couldn't get enough of him. Her hands roamed over his back, feeling the supple length of his spine, the solid columns of muscle, the sweatshirt. She pushed it out of the way and her hands found skin, hot, dry skin, burning with passion, smooth as silk and gliding over the underlying muscles.

She wanted more—much more. So did he, but he pulled away, lifting his head and cradling her chin under his.

'We have to stop,' he murmured gruffly.

'No.'

'Sarah, I don't have any condoms.'

Iced water couldn't have been more effective.

He was going back to Canada in eight weeks, and there was no way a pregnancy figured in either of their plans.

Her hands dropped to her sides and she stepped back, her body trembling in reaction. 'Good job one of us has got some common sense.'

Her voice sounded scratchy and unused.

'There's always tomorrow.'

Her eyes flew up and locked with his. 'Tomorrow?' she said weakly.

'Or I could go and find a pub with a dispenser in the gents'.'

But the mood was gone.

'No.' She stepped back. 'No, I don't think so—tempting though it is. Emily's here as well, don't forget.'

'I never forget Emily,' he said softly. 'I'll ask Ryan to have her tomorrow night.'

'Tomorrow—'

'Tomorrow. Or don't you want to?'

She was silent for a moment, her mind whirling. One thought came repeatedly to the surface. If he went back to Canada in eight weeks and she'd let this opportunity for fleeting happiness pass her by, would she regret it?

Yes.

She smiled shyly. 'Tomorrow sounds good,' she murmured.

His breath left his body in a slow, careful sigh. 'Right. In that case, I think you should go to bed, Sarah, before I change my mind about being noble.'

She went, almost running, and curled up in her bed thinking about the kiss and what would happen tomorrow.

She didn't sleep a wink.

CHAPTER SEVEN

ANTICIPATION was the most wonderful thing. By six o'clock the following evening when Matt left to take Emily to the O'Connors', he was ready to tear his hair out.

He'd been shopping for all sorts of delicacies, ignoring traditional aphrodisiacs like oysters and avocado in favour of lots of sensuous finger-foods, creamy dips and little fingers of crunchy fresh vegetables—nothing too heavy, nothing that would weigh on the stomach and distract them from the gentle art of seduction.

And to wash it down a fine, light wine, soft and fruity and bursting on the palate—a symphony of sensation.

He had in mind a sort of Bacchanalian feast, with them lying around feeding each other little nibbles of this and that—and clothes didn't feature too largely in his scheme either.

He was assailed by nerves, which was ridiculous, but perhaps he'd never played for such high stakes before. And they were high stakes. Unbelievably high.

He scrubbed a hand round the back of his neck and sighed. He hadn't meant to do this. He really hadn't. He had very strong principles about mixing business with pleasure, and Sarah Cooper was definitely business.

Damn.

He still couldn't walk away from her. There was something there that was too powerful to ignore, too rare to disregard. He needed her in a way he'd never needed anyone, and he had a strange and almost scary feeling that it was love.

112

He put the car away in the garage, closed the door and walked slowly up the path. Now the time was here he felt almost sick with anticipation. He wasn't sure he could eat. He wasn't sure he could do anything! He gave a hollow laugh. That would be a classic, if he was so nervous he couldn't perform!

He slipped his key into the lock and went in, listening. The house was silent except for the sound of running water.

Sarah was in the shower.

Heat slammed into him at the thought, and he went into the kitchen and started setting out the meal. He laid trays with little bowls full of his tempting morsels, checked the temperature of the wine and found two glasses.

They wouldn't need plates to feed each other.

He heard her footsteps on the stairs, coming down.

Oh, Lord. His eyes closed and he leant on the table with head down, telling himself to breathe slowly. Then he lifted his head and looked at her, and felt as if he'd been punched in the gut.

Sarah hovered in the kitchen doorway. She'd showered and washed her hair while Matt was out, and she hadn't realised he was back. She'd slipped down to the kitchen for a glass of iced water and there he was, standing in front of a tray of all sorts of things, head bowed, looking for all the world like a man about to be executed.

And then he lifted his head and saw her there in her underwear, and she felt the shock of his gaze right down to her toes.

Colour flooded her cheeks. 'I didn't realise you were back—I'll go and get dressed,' she said in a rush.

'Sarah, wait.'

She turned back again, fighting the urge to cover herself. She felt suddenly shy, very naked and vulnerable and lacking in confidence. Still, at least she was wearing her decent underwear!

'Take this,' he said, and held out a tray.

The bowls rattled against each other, and she realised with a start that he was nervous too.

'Take it where?'

'Upstairs.'

Their eyes clashed, then she reached out and took the tray from him, turned and climbed the stairs without a word.

'My room,' he instructed as she reached the top, and she pushed open the door and stopped.

It was immaculate, everything put away, the bed plump with fresh linen, and on every surface stood a candle. It was like a stage set, she thought—set for her seduction—and she was suddenly horribly unsure that she could do this, that he would want her when it came to the crunch.

He put the tray on the bed and lit the candles, then turned out the top light, leaving them bathed in the flickering golden glow of the flames.

'Here, let me take that.'

His voice was gruff, scratchy, and his hands shook. It gave her back her confidence. She smiled and reached out, touching his arm.

'You look a little over-dressed for this party,' she teased him gently.

Without a word he toed off his shoes, peeled his sweater over his head and then reached for his jeans. The rasp of the zip jammed her breath in her throat, and then he slid his jeans down, hooking off his socks *en route*, stealing the last of her air. All he wore were those sexy boxers of his, and a crooked and self-conscious smile.

Silly. They'd both seen each other in this little before, so why make such a fuss?

Because they knew where it was leading, of course.

He took her hand and led her to the bed, sitting her down and going round the other side to lie sprawled, the trays between them.

'Here. Try this.'

He dipped a thin stick of raw carrot in a dip and held it out to her. She bit it, and he dipped it again and ate the rest.

'Nice dip,' she murmured. 'What is it?'

'I have no idea. Try this one.'

They tried them all, their eyes locked on each other's lips, their tongues chasing little escapee drips of dip, deliberately teasing each other.

'Wine?' he murmured.

It was delicious, a fruity, sparkling wine that burst on the tongue like an explosion of sensation, bubbles racing over the inside of her mouth, sensitising it still further.

'Sarah?'

She opened her eyes and saw raw desire etched on his face.

'I need you.'

She slid off the bed, taking the trays and putting them on the floor just in reach, then turned back the quilt. 'I thought you'd never ask,' she said softly.

He joined her under the quilt, his hands cradling her cheeks, his mouth urgent. It was a wild kiss, much wilder than the one the night before, but there was no stopping this one. It was like a runaway train and it would demolish any argument in its path.

There were no arguments. They reached for each other, fumbling the last scraps of clothing aside then lying close without moving, just getting used to the overload of sensation the contact brought.

Her hands moved first, gliding over his skin, relishing the contrast between the soft silky texture and the taut muscle underneath. He was as tense as a bowstring, she thought, stroking the length of his spine. So tense. So needy.

'Matt?'

He opened his eyes and slid one hand under the pillow, coming out with a little foil packet. He handed it to her. 'I'll let you do the honours,' he said gruffly.

Her fingers fumbled helplessly. 'I can't do this,' she said, laughing, and he took over, holding his hands over hers and guiding her. Then he reached for her, and with a little sob she gave herself to him.

The climax shocked them both. Afterwards they lay silent for a while, just holding each other and waiting for the trembling to stop.

'Are you OK?' he asked eventually.

She smiled and touched his cheek. 'I think so. You?'

His grin was crooked and very dear. 'I'll get over it with practice.'

She laughed. 'Good.'

He disappeared for a moment to the bathroom, then plumped the pillows and lifted the trays back onto the bed, sliding in beside her. 'Right. I'm starving. I haven't eaten a thing all day.'

'Nor have I. I've been so scared.'

'Of me?' he asked, looking shocked.

'Of us. Of this. Of you not wanting me.'

His jaw dropped. 'Not wanting you? Are you crazy?'

She laughed self-consciously. 'I'm hardly a scrawny supermodel.'

'Oh, Sarah.' He cupped her cheek and turned her face to his, scattering soft kisses over her cheeks and lips. 'I didn't want to go to bed with a scrawny supermodel. I wanted to go to bed with you.'

'You say all the right things.'

He smiled wickedly. 'Of course. Eat this.'

He fed her a grape dipped in cream cheese. It was too indirect. She dipped her finger into the taramasalata and held it out to him. He sucked it, curling his tongue round it and suckling it rhythmically, his eyes locked with hers.

Then he took a dollop of something and smeared it over one of her nipples. She could hardly breathe for anticipation. His head lowered, his mouth closing hotly over the quivering peak.

He suckled hard, not hard enough to hurt but hard enough to make her cry out. He lifted his head and met her eyes silently, then repeated it with the other breast. It wasn't enough. He shifted the trays, threw the quilt aside and systematically used his mouth to drive her out of her mind. There hardly seemed a part of her he didn't caress with that clever, wicked tongue.

He even suckled her toes.

Then he worked his way back up again, and by the time he reached her mouth she was at fever pitch.

'That was just for starters,' he murmured. 'Want the main course?'

'Well, I'm not going on a diet now,' she said unevenly, laughter breaking in her voice, and he smiled and kissed her tenderly.

'Good.'

It was even better the second time—and the third, and the fourth.

They woke at some time in the night to find the candles burnt down and the quilt lying in a tray of dips, and decamped to her bedroom. In the morning they shared the shower, which was interesting as it was only small, and it made it very cosy.

Then they cleared up the mess in the other bedroom,

changed the sheets, tidied her room and went to collect
Emily.

Sarah sat in the car while he went in, not at all in a
hurry to face Ginny's good-natured ribbing and Ryan's
sly winks, however well intentioned their matchmaking
was. Sarah knew it was only going to be a temporary
fling. She didn't like it, and it would kill her when he
went, but she knew it was going to happen and nothing
Ryan and Ginny had to say about it would make any
difference.

Her main concern was to keep Emily out of the picture
as far as possible, so the innocent child wasn't hurt by
their foolishness.

Because it *was* foolishness, and neither of them could
deny it.

Still, it was worth it, every second of it, she thought.
Nothing could take last night away from her, or this
morning, when he'd been warm and sleepy and gruffly
tender, the rasp of his beard chafing her in all sorts of
places—

'Hi, sweetheart. Have a fun night?'

Emily fairly bounced into the car. 'Yeah, great. We
had a video. It was very silly. Even Ryan and Ginny
liked it, and Ginny made popcorn in the microwave, and
we all lay in a row—Ryan called us the Rugrats!'

Sarah and Matt met each other's eyes across the car
and smiled. At least they didn't have to feel guilty. They
went for a walk in the park again and fed the ducks and
Emily bumped into a schoolfriend in the playground.
Then they had to make tracks because Sarah was on duty
for the late shift. They had a quick lunch—of leftovers,
complete with memories that should have made their
hair curl—and Sarah left them to it and went to work.

She couldn't believe it was only forty-eight hours
since she'd last been there. It seemed far longer, with

everything that had happened, and she was sure her face
must show the changes in her life.

Apparently not. At least, if it did, no one said anything, which was highly unlike the motley crew she
worked with!

'Letter came for you by hand,' the receptionist said,
and handed it to her. She slipped it into her pocket until
she'd finished her stint in Triage, then when it all quie-
tened down again she went into the staffroom, made a
cup of tea and opened the envelope.

'It's from Jo,' she told Patrick, who was covering for
Jo over the weekend until something could be arranged.
She scanned the quick note and smiled sadly. 'Poor girl.
She's gone home with her mother for now. It's just a
quick thank-you for saving her life...'

She passed the note to Patrick and blew her nose,
scrubbing her cheeks on the back of her hands.

'Softy,' he murmured.

She sniffed and laughed. 'Don't let her hear you say
that. She thinks I'm as hard as nails.'

He made a rude noise and handed the note back. 'You
OK? You look a bit tired.'

She struggled to keep her face straight. 'No, I'm fine.
Late night.'

'Doing anything special?'

She felt the colour creeping into her cheeks, and
headed for the door, abandoning her half-cup of tea. 'Not
really. Lying around eating, mostly.'

'A lazy evening in, eh?' Patrick murmured, and she
knew her cover was blown. Oh, well, he could be trusted
not to talk.

'Must fly. Busy, busy, busy.'

His snort followed her down the corridor, and Sarah
wished she'd stayed and finished her tea. The department
was dead, the most exciting case in the waiting room

being raging dyspepsia from too much Sunday lunch. Busy, busy, busy, indeed!

She changed a dressing, plastered a back-slab that had come in for a new cast, repaired a broken cast, cut away and replaced part of a soggy one, did a couple of tiny stitches and wondered if her salary was justified.

Yeah, sure it was. Last week she'd more than earned it—and, anyway, after last night she was too tired to concentrate on anything more taxing.

Patrick was glad of a quiet day as well. He'd been up all night with the children, who'd eaten something which had made them sick. 'Anna did most of it, but you know what it's like with kids—if one's up, you're all up.'

'I remember,' she said with a smile. 'Emily's like that. If she wakes up in the morning, we all have to be awake. She comes and climbs into bed with me if there's time, and at the weekends Matt brings us all up breakfast in bed.'

'Cosy,' Patrick teased. 'I take it having her about doesn't cramp your style, then?'

She coloured furiously. 'Of course not! There's nothing to cramp!'

'So what did you mean, he "brings us all up breakfast in bed"?'

'Just that—he brings it up on a tray, and sits on the bed.' That immediately brought back memories of last night on a tide of added colour.

'Hey, I wasn't prying,' Patrick said hastily. 'It's time you had some fun, and Matt's a nice guy. I was just going to offer to babysit, if it helps. I can remember what it's like trying to have a relationship with a child on the scene.'

He was a sweetheart. She smiled at him, touched at his kindness. 'Thanks—but most of the time she goes to Ryan and Ginny,' she said, and then blushed furiously and stamped her foot in frustration. 'Oh, rats, I didn't mean that the way it came out!'

She laughed, and Patrick chuckled and patted her on the shoulder. 'Just enjoy yourself, and to hell with having to explain it to anyone.'

She shook her head in disbelief at the way he'd seen straight through her. 'It's only short term, anyway. He's got to go back to Canada in eight weeks.'

It was a sobering thought, and with her face like an open book it took Patrick scant seconds to realise she was going to be devastated.

'I'll be here for you,' he said quietly. 'Don't forget to lean, if you want. No one's an island.'

'You're a love, Patrick. Anna's a lucky woman.'

She hugged him, blinked away the tears and went to find the next set of patient notes before she broke down and howled her eyes out all over him.

The next couple of weeks were a joy and a strain, simultaneously. A joy because every moment she managed to snatch alone with Matt was wonderful, and a strain because either their colleagues or Emily were watching over their shoulders most of the time.

And nights, with Emily in the house, were a definite no-no.

At least they were both in agreement about that, so they contented themselves with long cuddles on the sofa and kisses that left them both climbing walls.

Matt decided they needed time to themselves on Valentine's Day, and so he booked a table in a restaurant, arranged for Emily to go to Ryan and Ginny again for the night, and told Sarah to stand by for the night of her life.

Sarah laughed. 'I've already had the night of my life.

Whatever you do, nothing else will ever be the first time
again.'

'Ah, but I can top it.'

'One day,' she warned, 'your vanity will get you in
trouble. And anyway, I'm on duty until six.'

'But I'm not, so I'll be nicely rested!'

'Nicely rested for what, or shouldn't one ask?' Ryan
murmured, coming up behind them.

'One shouldn't ask,' Matt told him bluntly.

'Oh. Right. That.' He grinned and walked off, leaving
Sarah a very pretty shade of pink, and Matt chuckling.

'You're outrageous. I think we should change the subject.'

'Me too. All this talk and no action is driving me
crazy.'

He strode off, whistling softly, to carry on with his
next patient, and Sarah took his last through to the plaster room to put on a back-slab. It was Friday, and she
was on duty right through till Sunday evening.

But then, of course, she had Monday off, so she could
sleep all day if necessary! Chattering happily to the little
boy to put him and his mum at their ease, she spread
the padded gauze over the child's wrist, squeezed out
the plaster bandages and smoothed them on, leaving a
gap up the inside in case the limb swelled up in the
night. Once it was set she put the sling on, ruffled his
hair and sent him off with his mother.

He was seven, about the age James would have been,
she thought, and had a sudden pang of longing. She
hoped they were all right, wherever they were.

And her baby—Helen's baby—who even after all this
time she still never called by a name. How could she?
She didn't even know her name. Was she all right, out
there in the world somewhere with Brad and Helen?

She couldn't have been more loved, Sarah reminded herself, or more wanted.

Wanted by all of them.

'You OK?'

She drew in a deep breath and met Matt's eyes. 'Yes. Just a bit of time-travelling.'

'Ah, sweetheart—'

'RTA coming in on a blue light. Stand by, everyone!'

'Save me a hug,' she murmured, and went to prepare Resus. 'What do we know?'

'Woman and two children—children apparently unrestrained, preschool age. One child head injuries, the other breathing difficulties. The woman's got chest and head injuries and possible fracture of humerus. No one else involved,' Jack told her. 'I want a team on each, initially, until we can see how it's going.'

'Right.' Two unrestrained preschool children. Sarah forced herself to be dispassionate. 'It's none of your business,' she muttered.

'I never said a word!'

'Oh—hi, Patrick. Jack wants three teams in Resus—three coming in from an RTA, woman and two small children—unrestrained.'

He said something unprintable, then headed towards Resus. Sarah carried on to the nursing station. 'Can I have four nurses, please, for Resus, stat. RTA coming in.'

'Do you really need me?' one asked. 'Only I promised to go via the supermarket and I've been late off every night this week, and I know we won't get away until they're sorted, and I really do need to get off on time tonight.'

'And I'm due off in twenty minutes, too, and I missed lunch.'

She swivelled round to the last three. 'Your excuses?'

They dropped everything and came. She rounded up another on the way back, and warned the triage nurse that they were going to be blowing the waiting-time target to pieces yet again. Then a blue flicker appeared over the cars in the car park and the first ambulance pulled up at the doors, disgorging its little victims.

They were so small they were on the same stretcher, end to end, one pinched and bluish and coughing weakly, the other silent and pale. The one with the cough was tilted downhill slightly.

'No names as yet,' Tom Hallam of the dog bite told Sarah as he wheeled them in. 'The little one hit the windscreen, the boy must have inhaled something but there's only partial obstruction so we've given one hundred per cent oxygen and just got here fast. We haven't tried chest thrusts because of any possible trauma from the crash.'

'And the mother?'

'She's on her way. Doesn't look wonderful.'

'Right. Thanks, Tom.'

She and Matt got the child with the chest, the older one—probably about three or four, Sarah guessed, yet another little boy who put her in a time warp. He was trying to cough and cry, and Matt encouraged him to cough hard, but the next inhalation just made it worse again.

'Do you know what you swallowed, my love?' Sarah asked, getting down on his level. 'Was it a sweetie?'

He nodded, and in between broken breaths he said, 'I want—my mummy!'

'I think we need to move to a cubicle,' Matt said to Jack. 'I've given him a cursory check and he seems unscathed—Mum coming in with major trauma won't be an asset to our young friend, not to mention the sibling.'

'Good idea. Pupils reactive—good. Can we get a

GCS?' He glanced up at them for a moment. 'Try chest thrusts.'

'I shall—once I've checked ribs and sternum and looked down his throat a bit more thoroughly.'

They went into a cubicle and, by using a teddy first, Matt persuaded the little boy to let him examine him. 'I'm listening to Teddy's chest—oh, that sounds good! Can I listen to yours? I can? Thank you. Oh, yes, I can hear that. That's very good. Well done, what a brave boy! Can you say "Ah" for me, like this, and stick your tongue out? Ah-h-h—good, that's great.'

'Anything?' Sarah asked.

'I think it's high up. The wheezing's in the lower part of the pharynx or the larynx—no lower, I don't think. I can't see it, though. I wonder if we upend and thump—?'

'Could try.'

He checked the rest of the child rapidly, especially any abdominal signs that might have been missed, and any sign of head injury, in case there was some slow but potentially fatal bleed brewing somewhere. Then Matt sat down with his legs tucked underneath the chair so his lap was sloping, they placed the child face-down across his lap so his head was going downhill, and with the edge of his hand Matt gave five sharp blows to the little boy's back, just between the shoulder-blades.

Then he propped him up, did five sharp upward thrusts to the chest with his arms round him and the child's back against his chest, and with the last thrust a sweet flew out and shot across the room.

The little boy started to gasp and cry in earnest, and Matt gathered him in his arms, rocked him gently and soothed him.

It didn't work. Sarah would have loved it, but the little boy wasn't hers, and he wanted his mummy. Sarah, soft and womanly, would have to do. She gathered him up into her arms, sat down and cradled him against her bosom, and little by little his frantic cries slowed and stopped.

'He's asleep,' Matt told her.

'I know. I'll stay with him. Go and see how the others are.'

He was gone a minute or two, then came back to report that the little girl with head injuries didn't look serious at the moment, although she had some lovely bruises, but the young woman who'd been driving was in a serious condition.

'Her chest seems to be the worst—she wasn't wearing a seat belt either, and she's impacted with the steering wheel at speed. Oh, and they don't think she's the mother. She's got no rings, she's wearing shabby clothes and the children are both really well dressed. The car was pretty rough, apparently, and the girl seems very young to have two children this age. They think she might be the nanny, but police are checking now. Certainly she's not married, whatever.'

Sarah looked down at the poor little mite in her arms, and wondered if he knew his name and address. That was something her boys had had drummed into them from an early age.

It seemed a shame to wake him, but he was calm now and might cope better. She stroked his cheek. 'Wake up, sleepyhead.'

His eyes flickered and drifted shut, and then as she continued stroking, they opened again and he looked up at her in confusion. 'Remember me? I'm the nurse. We got your sweetie out of your throat.'

He nodded, and his lip wobbled. 'Want Mummy,' he mumbled.

'Was she in the car?'

He shook his head.

'So was that your nanny?'

He nodded.

'Well, we want to find your mummy so you can see her, but we don't know where to look first. Can you be a very clever boy and help us find her?'

The lad nodded, his eyes like saucers.

'First of all, can you tell us your name, and where you live?'

'Michael Smith, 14 Warrington Avenue, Audley, Suffolk,' he said, parrot-fashion.

'Clever boy! Well done! And what's your sister called, Michael?'

'Taran Elizabeth.'

'Right. Now, if we go and ask a nice policeman, do you think he'll be able to go round to your house and find your mummy there, or does she go to work?' Sarah asked, her fingers crossed behind his back.

'She goes shopping on Friday.'

So far, so good. Shopping shouldn't take that long.

'Tell you what, let's go and find a policeman and tell him where you live, Michael, and he can start to find Mummy, OK?'

Michael nodded, snuggling against Sarah's shoulder, and she tucked an arm firmly under his bottom and stood up. Gosh, he was heavy. She found the policemen in the staffroom, drinking tea, while they waited to speak to the nanny.

'This is Michael, gentlemen,' she said, smoothing back his hair off his brow and smiling at him. 'He was in the car with his sister and his nanny. Michael's a very clever boy because he knows his name and address. Can you tell the policemen where you live?'

He could, and he was still feeling obliging, so Sarah

left the two men in charge of trying to contact his mother and started filling in forms with their details.

'When's your birthday, Michael? I bet you can't remember!'

'The twenty-sixth of September.'

'And how old are you now?'

'Four. I go to school after the summer,' he said proudly.

'I expect you'll enjoy that as you're so clever. Lots to do.'

'Tara won't be able to go,' Michael told her seriously, 'because she's only two. She's not three until June, so she can't go till the next year, and Elizabeth's just a baby.'

'Elizabeth?' Something wasn't right here.

'Taran Elizabeth', he'd said—or had he said 'Tara *and* Elizabeth'?

'My baby sister. Where is she?' he twisted round, looking for her. 'Where's Tara 'n' Elizabeth?'

Sarah had a ghastly sinking feeling.

'Michael, how many sisters do you have?' she asked. 'Two.'

'And was Elizabeth with you in the car?' she said calmly.

'Mmm. She kept screaming and crawling around. Nicole turned round to stop her, and then the car went bang and I swallowed my sweetie.'

And Elizabeth disappeared.

Oh, Lord.

Sara scooped him up and went to find the policemen who by now were in the office on the phone. 'Um— Michael tells me he's got two sisters, and little baby Elizabeth was in the car too, so while you're looking for Mum, could you see if you can find where she's got to?' she asked with a rather frantic little smile. 'She's crawling, isn't she, Michael, so she might have gone off by herself to explore, and we wouldn't want her to get lost, would we, chaps?'

They were gone, almost before she'd finished speaking, the details relayed down the phone already and presumably notified to officers already on the scene. The two of them had gone to join in the search, confident that the nanny was going nowhere for a while and would still be there for questioning later.

Mrs Smith came in just a few minutes later, hurrying in with arms outstretched, and Sarah relinquished her delighted charge gladly. He hadn't wanted to be put down, but after all that time he was getting somewhat heavy, and he was tying up Sarah who should have been doing something more useful.

Like telling someone that one of her children is unaccounted for?

'How are the others?' Mrs Smith asked frantically. 'Can I see them? Where are they? She knows she's not allowed to take them in her car!'

'Tara's in another room—they're just checking her over and making sure she's stable. She had a bump on the head. I'll find the doctor who's been working on her to come and talk to you.'

'And Elizabeth? How's Elizabeth? Where is she?'

Mrs Smith's voice was beginning to rise in panic when Sarah heard a firm, heavy stride approaching.

'Is this what you're looking for?' the ambulance man asked, and handed Sarah a nine-month-old baby, cold, wet, muddy, but very much alive and still quite cheerful.

She shot him a brilliant smile. 'Thanks. She went missing at the scene. We didn't know she was in the car until Michael told us all about it—he's a clever boy. You should be proud of him.' She looked down at the squirming baby. 'I think we'd just better check this little one out for lumps and bumps but she seems fine. What a lucky escape, poppet. Yes, it was!'

The baby gurgled, and Sarah thought she'd scream if she had to treat one more child today. So many memories...so much emptiness...

Matt appeared at her elbow. 'Tara's doing well—do you want Jack?'

'Please—and then can you come and check her little sister?'

'Sister?' he mouthed as he walked backwards down the corridor, out of sight of the mother. He turned and went into Resus, appearing moments later with Jack. Michael was placed on the chair 'to keep the baby company', Jack took Mrs Smith off to see Tara, and they were left alone with the children.

'Sister?' Matt said again.

'Mmm—she was thrown clear and crawled off. Lucky little scamp. Could you check her out?'

She was, amazingly, fine.

Sarah and Matt weren't. They were hours late getting home yet again, but it was unavoidable. There were some cases you could hand over, and others you couldn't. The Smiths had been one of those.

Tara was stable and improving, the other two were obviously fine and only the nanny remained on the critical list.

Sarah found it very hard to be sympathetic, but at least fate had worked in the children's favour and not the other way this time. That would have been really difficult to swallow.

They went home and put a tired and crotchety Emily to bed, and then Sarah herself turned in shortly afterwards, worn out by the emotion of the day. There was another day tomorrow, she thought, and another one on Sunday, and then she and Matt could have their stolen evening together.

If she lasted that long!

CHAPTER EIGHT

THE best laid plans, and all that.

Evie O'Connor had flu on Sunday, and so Emily couldn't go to them. Matt tried the babysitter, but she was already booked up, and he was forced to cancel their dinner.

'Let's just get a take-away and eat it after Emily goes to bed,' Sarah suggested. 'She's looking peaky anyway. I expect she could do with an early night.'

Matt grimaced ruefully and cupped her cheek. 'I could have done with an early night,' he told her. An early night and a chance to say all the things that he had to say to her, without the possibility of any interruptions. So much hung in the balance, and there was a little square box in his jacket pocket all ready, just in case.

He could have screamed with frustration. He might have done, if there hadn't been a little bit of him that was secretly relieved. He was nervous—even more nervous than he'd been the first night, but there was more at stake now.

And he'd had a stay of execution.

He gave a silent, bitter laugh. He was going to ask her to marry him, so why did it feel like a trip to the gallows?

Whatever, it wouldn't happen tonight, in a candlelit restaurant with discreet waiters and soft music and all the other clichés. Maybe that was better. Perhaps he'd sit down with Sarah tonight and tell her he loved her and ask her to marry him—

'Matt? Are you OK?'

He dredged up a smile and stroked her cheek with his thumb. 'Yeah, I'm fine.'

Her hand came up and covered his. 'I know it's disappointing, but there'll be other times. We'll have to take a lunch-break together or something.' Her grin was mischievous and he loved her.

'Sure.'

He hugged her. She thought tonight was just some big seduction set-up. She didn't have the slightest clue...

Sarah was disappointed. She'd been looking forward to having Matt to herself again. It had seemed such a long time, and she'd so enjoyed just being able to hold him, without having eyes in the back of her head.

Never mind. As she'd said to him, there'd be other times.

While Matt went out for the take-away, she bathed Emily and tucked her up in bed, sitting up beside her to read her a story. It was lovely snuggling with her, she thought, and the fact that they were leaving in only six weeks didn't bear thinking about. She opened the book and tried to concentrate, as Emily cuddled in against her side and pointed to the pictures.

'"And they all lived happily ever after." There. What a lovely story.' Sarah closed the book and put it down, and looked at Emily. Was she asleep? No, not quite, but almost. She stood up and snuggled Emily down under the quilt, kissed her cheek and was just going out when a little voice stopped her.

'My mummy used to kiss me goodnight like that,' Emily said quietly. 'I miss her.'

'Oh, Emily.' She went back to the bedside, crouching down and smoothing the heavy dark hair back from the child's face. She wanted to weep for her. Words were just so inadequate—

'Sarah?'

'Mmm?'

Emily reached for her hand and held it trustingly. 'Sarah, would you like to be my new mummy?'

Her heart lurched. 'Oh, sweetheart, of course I would, more than you can know, but you and Daddy have to go back to Canada soon—'

'But I don't want to! I don't want to leave you.'

'Oh, darling.' Sarah leaned over and drew the little girl into her arms. 'Sometimes we have to do things we don't want to do, but usually it's because in the end it's the best thing. And, anyway, I can always come and see you,' she promised rashly, knowing that when Matt went back that would be the end of it.

'Will you? Will you come?' Emily pleaded.

'Yes—I promise.'

And may God strike me down for lying to a child, she thought wretchedly, because there was no way she and Matt could sustain a relationship over thousands of miles of ocean. She straightened.

'You go to sleep now, sweetheart. You're looking tired.'

'I am. Night, Sarah.'

'Goodnight, poppet.'

She pulled the door to and went into her own room, closing the door firmly and sitting down on the bed while she struggled with tears. She'd love to be Emily's mummy, she thought—and Matt's wife—but he hadn't asked her, and he was still talking about going back to Canada soon.

She didn't think she could bear to lose anyone else.

She stood up and took the photo albums out of the top of her wardrobe, and opened them. Such happy photos.

They'd had a good marriage, she thought, looking at Rob laughing into the camera. He'd been kind and thoughtful and generous—a little untidy, but you couldn't have everything and the rest had more than compensated.

At least the boys had been secure and happy, she thought, even if their lives had been brutally cut short. They'd never known fear or hunger or danger, never been neglected or unwanted or unloved.

She wondered what it was like for Emily to have a mother who didn't care, and her heart ached for the little scrap.

'Sarah?'

'Come in.'

'Are you OK?'

She looked up at Matt and thought how dear he'd become to her in so short a time. 'Yes, I'm fine,' she said, and closed the book.

He nodded his head towards it. 'What's that?'

'Photos of Rob and the boys, and a couple of the baby. I'll show you later, if you like. Did you get the take-away?'

'Yes.' He looked thoughtful, as if there was something he wanted to say, but then he turned and went out.

She followed him and paused in Emily's doorway. 'She went down like a lamb.'

'Good. Come and eat.'

They went downstairs and took the take-away cartons through to the dining room. Matt had laid the table with candles and red napkins to give a romantic feel to it, but it didn't feel quite right. There was something wrong with him, she thought. He seemed tense, as if something was on his mind, and it was a relief really when the meal was over and they could go into the sitting room.

'Come and sit here,' he said, patting the sofa beside him. 'I want to talk to you.'

So there was something, she thought, sitting down carefully beside him—but what?

He put his arm round her and held her closer, but for a long time he was silent.

'Matt?'

She felt his chest rise, as if he'd taken a deep breath, and then he began. His voice sounded tight and a little strained, and she realised he was nervous.

'When I took this job it was strictly short term,' he began. 'I never thought for a moment that I would end up wanting to stay, but I've enjoyed working here, and Emily's settled, and—well, the fact is that Jack's told me he's switching to an ITU post in a few months, and that creates a vacancy.'

'Jack's leaving?'

'Yes. It's all strictly hush-hush at the moment, but I'm sure he wouldn't mind me telling you. Anyway, the point is that he told me the job's mine if I want it, but that all rather depends on you.'

'Me?' A warm feeling started up around her heart, but she made herself wait and hear him out.

'Yes, you.' He shifted a little so he was facing her, and his eyes were troubled but sincere. 'I liked you the moment I first met you, but then I expected to, really. I'd heard a lot about you, about the sort of person you were, and I didn't expect you to be difficult to get along with. What I also didn't expect, which really took me by surprise, was how easy it would be to fall in love with you.'

'Oh, Matt.' Her hand came up and cupped his craggy jaw, and she reached up and pressed a kiss to his other cheek.

He took her hands in his, holding them like a lifeline, and continued, 'This is only the third time in my life I've ever done this, so you'll have to forgive me if I fluff my lines. The first time I was five, so that doesn't really count, and the second was a disaster.' He looked down. 'This one really matters, though, not just to me, but to Emily, because this affects her too, more than you realise.'

'She asked me tonight if I could be her new mummy,' Sarah told him, and then wondered if she were jumping the gun and if he had actually been getting round to asking her that.

'And what did you say?' he asked tensely.

'That I'd love to, but you were going back to Canada and it would be very difficult, but that I'd still come and see her.'

'And would you?'

'That would depend. If you went back and there was someone else in your life, then maybe not. I'd write to her, though, and I'd miss her, whatever.'

'What if you didn't have to miss her—or me? What if there was a way we could be together?'

She smiled in relief. So she hadn't been wrong. 'Together?' she coaxed.

'Ah, hell,' he muttered, and sliding off the edge of the sofa he turned towards her on his knees and took her hands again. 'Sarah Cooper, I love you, more than I can say, and I'd be honoured and privileged if you'd consent to be my wife. How's that?'

She laughed, joy bursting inside her and filling her with hope. 'Wonderful—and, yes, I'd be delighted.'

He seemed to crumple. 'Thank God for that.' He fished in his pocket and pulled out a little box, then flipped the lid and lifted out a ring. It was very simple, almost plain, just a row of diamonds set in a Victorian setting, and he slid it onto her finger and sighed with relief.

'Amazing—it fits! I pinched one of your others for the size.'

She laughed in sheer delight and held it up, turning it this way and that so that the stones sparkled in the light. 'Oh, Matt,' she whispered, choked, and he reached for her.

She slid to her knees beside him. 'You're supposed to kiss me,' she told him, and with a strangled laugh he lowered his head and kissed her thoroughly, then he tucked her head back under his chin again and held her close against his heart.

'You are sure?' he asked after an age.

'Of course I'm sure. I love you to bits, Matthew Jordan, and your daughter, so if you've changed your mind, tough.'

He gave a wry little laugh. 'Oh, no, I haven't changed my mind. Far from it. It's just that I wanted you to be very sure, because—'

The sound of the doorbell cut through the quiet house like a siren.

'Who on earth can that be?' Sarah exclaimed.

Matt sighed shortly. 'I don't know, but their timing's lousy. Would you like to get rid of them? We still have a lot to talk about, and I really want some time alone with you.'

'Give me two ticks,' she said with a smile, and, scrambling to her feet, she went and opened the front door.

'Mum? Dad?'

'Hello, darling,' her mother said, stepping over the threshold, immaculate as ever and looking incredibly well. 'We've just got back from our cruise, and I thought we'd pop in and tell you all about it. How are you?'

Sarah smiled and drew them into the hall, hugging

them both. 'Actually, I'm fine, and your timing's perfect. There's someone I want you to meet. Come on in.'

She led them into the sitting room, and was relieved to find Matt on his feet in the middle of the room, his hair roughly finger-combed into submission, and looking more or less respectable if a touch stunned.

'Matt, these are my parents, Brenda and Russell Wesley. Mum, Dad, this is Matt Jordan.'

Matt shook hands with them both, and they all launched into the social niceties and subtle inquisition that usually accompanied the first meeting of parents with their daughter's suitor, regardless of age or previous history. She could have been sixteen again, she thought fondly, and decided to rescue Matt, even though he was holding his own remarkably well.

'Matt, have we got any of that nice sparkling wine in the fridge?'

'The one we had the other night?' he suggested, bringing back a flood of inappropriate memories, and she nodded, suppressing a grin.

'I think there's another bottle. I'll fetch it.'

He went out, winking at her, and then Sarah, ever direct and to the point, said, 'I do hope you like him, because he's just asked me to marry him, and I've accepted.'

Brenda's mouth sagged for a brief second, and Russell cleared his throat and said, 'Ah. Um.' Matt came back in with a clutch of wine glasses dangling from one hand and a bottle of bubbly dangling from the other, straight into a stunned silence.

He looked at Sarah, she grinned and went and linked her arm through his, and then she turned to her parents and smiled. 'Congratulate us, then,' she prompted, and her parents seemed to come to life.

'Oh, darling,' her mother said mistily, and hugged her

hard. 'Oh, Sarah, I do hope you'll be happy. You deserve it more than anyone I know.'

'Oh, Mum, stuff and nonsense.'

'You do. And I like him—good eye contact. That's very important,' her father said, winking at Matt.

She laughed and went into her father's arms, accepting his bone-cracking hug without a murmur. He'd been devastated when Rob and the boys had died, and he'd been a tower of strength to her. A man of few words, he said nothing, just held her to let her know he was still there for her if she needed him.

'Matt, open the wine,' she suggested when her father released her.

The cork flew, the wine foamed and they all laughed and sipped and toasted.

And into the middle of it all walked Emily, chalk-faced and unsteady, with eyes like saucers, and announced calmly, 'Daddy, I've been sick—and I think I'm going to be sick again.'

It was funny how a little thing like a vomiting child could show people in their true colours, Sarah thought with a smile. She'd changed sheets and found fresh pyjamas, Matt had bathed Emily and put her back to bed, her father had sorted out the floor and her mother had taken off her smart jacket, rolled up her sleeves and put all the accident-damaged bedding in the washing machine.

Many parents, she knew, would have drained their glasses, stepped over the crisis on the carpet and left, promising to ring the next day.

Not Sarah's. They stayed as long as they could be useful, then they left, offering help if needed. 'He's nice,' they said *sotto voce* as they went out. 'Looking forward to meeting him properly—and Emily, poor little love.'

By the time the poor little love was settled it was nearly three in the morning, because she kept waking to be sick, and crying because her throat hurt.

Matt went to bed in the end, leaving Sarah mopping and sponging and telling little stories, because he had to go to work the next day and she had the day off.

'But it seems unfair,' he protested round a huge yawn, and she smiled and patted his cheek.

'If I'm going to be her mother, I might as well start now—and, anyway, it'll teach me not to volunteer for things rashly, won't it?'

He looked as if he was going to say something, but then he hugged her and went to bed.

In fact, Emily wasn't sick again, and once she seemed settled Sarah went to bed herself and left the door open so she could hear if Emily woke.

She didn't, and the next thing she was aware of was Matt, bringing her a cup of tea on his way out in the morning. ''Em looks better—she's cooler and her colour's more normal. Thank you so much for last night.'

She smiled and reached up and hugged him. 'My pleasure.'

'Will you be all right today?'

'Of course we will. I'll see you tonight. Oh, and by the way, my parents like you.'

He looked a little self-conscious. 'I'm glad. I liked them too. Maybe next time we'll get to have a whole conversation!' He leaned over and kissed her goodbye, then went out, checking Emily again on the way.

Sarah drank her tea, dozed for a little while and then showered and dressed. It was ages before Emily woke, totally exhausted by the night, and she and Sarah had a very quiet, lazy day in front of the television. It was the sort of day Sarah had had before, many times, and she found she slipped back into the channel-hopping and time-passing routine very easily.

They sang songs, had drinks and Sarah read stories. Emily lay very quietly and slept off and on, and all Sarah could think about was that she wasn't going to have to lose contact with this delightful little girl.

Or her father.

She missed Matt. It seemed a very long day, but finally he was home, tired, pale and complaining of a sore throat.

'Uh-oh,' Sarah said cautiously.

'Don't. I'm trying not to think about it, but I got rather close to her last night and I spent the whole day with her yesterday, so it would be a miracle if I didn't have it.'

'Early night?' she suggested.

'Good idea.'

'Have you eaten today?'

He pulled a face, and she sent him up to bed and brought him a glass of iced water.

'Just sip it,' she warned. 'If you try and drink it fast you'll lose it...'

'I'm not that bad—yet. I'm mainly staying out of your way.'

She laughed. 'Matt, I've spent the day with Emily. Don't you think that's rather closing the stable door after the horse has bolted?'

He smiled wryly. 'Very likely, but I'd still hate you to get it.'

'I don't want it either, so I'll say goodnight from here. Is there anything else you need?'

He grinned. 'Only a hug.'

'That'll have to wait. Sleep well—and, don't forget, sip, don't gulp.'

She went to bed herself not very late, and all was quiet in the house. Perhaps he hadn't got it, she thought, but in the morning she found he was hot, feverish and very sore.

'My throat's raw, my chest kills and I want to die.'

'That's the flu,' Sarah said cheerfully. 'Lots of rest, lots of fluids and don't let Emily bully you into reading to her. I'll tell her to look after you, and she'll probably spoil you rotten. Oh, and take aspirin.'

'Yes, mother,' he muttered.

She left him to it. He could wallow in self-pity much more effectively if she wasn't there!

It was chaos at work. Ryan was off, Matt was off and Jo, of course, was on long-term sick leave. That left Jack and Patrick and a couple of house doctors, who, while better than Jo, were still pretty junior and needed help on occasions.

The only good thing about it was her mood. Despite the chaos she was cheerful, buoyed up by the knowledge that Matt loved her and that they would be getting married.

Needless to say, Patrick didn't miss it. 'You're in a good mood,' he said with a searching look.

'I should be—Matt and I are getting married.'

Patrick gave a slow smile and hugged her fit to break her ribs. 'That's brilliant news. I thought he was looking pretty chipper yesterday. I take it this was before he got the flu.'

She laughed. 'Oh, yes—but as Emily got it. She threw up all over my parents as we were giving them the news.'

Patrick chuckled. 'How to win friends and influence people. I must try it some time.'

'Don't,' she pleaded. 'I've had more than enough of it. I've had two near misses today already!'

It didn't get better. They ran behind, they missed breaks and by the end of the day the last thing they needed was a known drug user brought in by a 'friend' in a state of collapse.

''Ere, 'e's got summink of mine and I wannit,' Sarah was told by the 'friend'. His voice was slurred, his eyes were wild and he was obviously going through withdrawal. He was cold and clammy, sweating, and very agitated. Sarah organised someone to sit him down with a cup of sweet tea, and alerted Patrick, filling him in as they hurried to Resus.

'Two young men—both known users. Our ''patient'' is called Charlie. I don't know about the other one—something odd. Anyway, he says Charlie's got something of his and, judging by the way he keeps guarding him, I think Charlie's bodypacking.'

'Oh, great. He's swallowed some damn condom full of cocaine or something and Oddball wants us to get it out intact, I suppose?'

She grinned. 'That's the one!'

'And what if we're too late?'

'Oh, I don't think we are. He's high as a kite but not too high, but if it bursts before we get it out, Charlie's going into orbit.'

'Narcotics or cocaine?'

'I'd say cocaine. He's talking a mile a minute—but, of course, that may not be what he's packing.'

'Any chest pain?'

'I haven't spoken to him yet, I've just heard him. I've got a porter holding him down at the moment. He seemed pretty lively.'

'I'm sure.' They went into Resus and found the porter struggling to persuade Charlie to lie still and wait.

'He'll kill me! You've got to be bloody joking, lie here! Here, are you the doctor? Thank God for that. Look, mate, you've got to help me. Pharaoh thinks I'm fooling, but I can't get this damn thing out! Look, I've got a bit of thread on it, but it won't come when I pull—see.'

And he stuck his fingers into his mouth, seized hold of the thread and tugged. 'Stuck, see? And he doesn't believe me! What the hell do I do? Get it out, Doc,' he pleaded.

'OK, let's have a look,' Patrick said calmly. 'Just lie still and let me see what's going on here. How are you feeling?'

'How am I feeling? What do you mean, how am I feeling? What is this, the bloody Women's Institute? He's going to kill me, mate!'

Patrick rolled his eyes and Sarah grinned, just out of sight. 'I'm not asking to be social. I want to know if you feel in any way abnormal.'

Charlie gave a high-pitched, rather manic laugh. 'Feel great. Best high I've had in years. You've got to help when I crash, though, 'cos it's going to be hell—'

'You got that out yet?' Pharaoh yelled through the door.

Alvin, the porter, went out to sit him down with another cup of tea, and Sarah and Patrick managed to get a blood-pressure cuff on Charlie.

'A bit high,' Patrick muttered. 'Charlie, I want to try and pull this thing out, and I want you to relax and just let it come, all right?'

He pulled on gloves, grasped the thread with his fingers and began to ease it out. 'Just cough for me, that's it—lovely.'

Charlie'd gagged and the condom flew out, still attached to the string around Charlie's tooth. Just then

Pharaoh barged in, saw the precious booty and grabbed for it.

The condom burst, scattering white powder everywhere, and Charlie screamed and clutched his face. Blood gushed from his mouth, and on the other end of the thread dangled a neatly extracted molar.

'You ought to take up dentistry, Pharaoh,' Patrick told him, but Pharaoh wasn't listening. He was kneeling on the floor at their feet, head down, sniffing up as much cocaine as he could before Security pounced on him.

'And to think they do it for kicks,' the security guard said drily as he wheeled the two of them away to escort them off the premises.

'So why was Charlie so high?' Sarah asked Patrick as they cleaned up the mess.

Patrick grinned. 'I don't think he could resist a little snort before he swallowed it. I also think he could quite easily have got it out on his own, but I think he was fooling around and was going to take it out later and keep it for himself—assuming Pharaoh didn't kill him and slit him open to get it.'

'Mad. They're all stark, staring mad. Right, I'm going home before anything else happens in this madhouse.'

'Oh, sweetheart, what's the matter?'

'I can't make the video work any more and I want my mummy,' she sobbed.

'Oh, darling!'

Sarah had come in to find Emily, crying on her own in the sitting room, the television fuzzy and no sign of Matt. She scooped the little one up, hugged her close and went to find him.

She didn't have to look far. He was lying flat on the bed, glistening with sweat, dressed only in those skimpy boxers and looking somewhat sick. He turned his head as she went in and his whole body seemed to sag with relief.

'Thank God you're back,' he croaked. 'I went downstairs to get Emily something to eat— Oh, hell—'

He stumbled off the bed, ran past her and fell into the bathroom.

'Daddy's being sick,' Emily said unnecessarily.

Sarah hid a smile. 'I noticed. I tell you what, let's take you back downstairs, give you some supper and a nice big drink, and then I'll change his sheets and give him a wash and maybe he'll feel better.'

'I did when you did that.'

'I know. It helps. Come on, then, let's sort you out first.'

He emerged from the bathroom, his eyes red-rimmed and his face chalky, and grimaced.

'You look rough. Go and lie on Em's bed for a while. I'll sort your sheets out.'

They went downstairs and Sarah made some toast and honey for Emily with a glass of lemon barley water, then she ran upstairs, changed the sheets, wheeled Matt back to bed, freshened him up and gave him some tepid electrolyte solution.

'Sadist,' he muttered, sipping it, and fell back on the pillows with a groan. 'I feel like death.'

'You look pretty good too. Can you keep aspirin down?'

The answer was not for long. Oh, well, it might have done some good. She left him in peace, hoping he'd sleep it off, and went back to Emily. She was asleep, crashed out on the sofa, exhausted after her bout of tears.

Sarah carried her up to bed, tucked her in, showered and dressed in a comfy old jogging suit and went downstairs again.

She didn't feel like eating much, so she made herself

toast and honey, took a pot of tea with her into the sitting room and curled up on the sofa. There was a video stuck in the mouth of the video player, one she didn't recognise, and she knelt down on the floor and looked at it.

'Emily, Christmas concert, Berlin. 3½,' it said on the label.

'Oh, wow.' She turned the television on again, wiggled the dodgy aerial wire in the back of the video player and pushed the cassette home.

It was a typical nursery school concert, with stage-struck children fluffing their lines. Emily was instantly recognisable, her little poem word-perfect except for one troublesome word, and Sarah laughed, sharing her triumph when the word was finally out.

She sang carols with the others, then at the end she broke ranks and ran towards the camera. 'Mummy, Daddy, I did it!' She giggled. 'Did you see me?'

'Sure we saw you,' a strangely familiar voice said.

The camera panned round, following the little girl as she ran up to her mother. 'Was I OK, Mummy?'

'You were wonderful. I love you.' The blonde woman bent forward, scooped Emily up and turned towards the camera, still laughing.

Sarah felt the blood drain from her face.

The woman with blonde hair, the one Emily had called Mummy, was Helen.

And Emily was her daughter.

CHAPTER NINE

IT WAS ages before Sarah could move.

The video finished playing and switched off, and still she sat there, staring blankly at the blizzard on the television screen.

Emily was her daughter.

She couldn't be.

She was. There was no other explanation.

But why, then, was she with Matt, and where were Brad and Helen?

And, come to that, who *was* Matt? A chill of fear began to seep over her.

Had he kidnapped Emily? Falsified references to get a job and come to England to be near Sarah? Lied his way into a relationship with her?

And, if so, why?

Blackmail?

Insurance fraud?

Murder?

Oh, Lord. She started to move then, finding her car keys, her handbag, the little stash of cash—there was no time to pack, just time to pick Emily up out of bed and carry her downstairs. She bundled her into the car and drove her round to Ryan and Ginny.

'Sarah? Whatever's the matter?' they asked.

'I can't explain. Just keep her here and, whatever you do, don't let Matt in. If you don't hear from me in two hours, call the police and send them round.'

'Police? Sarah, what are you talking about?' Ryan asked, confused. 'What's going on?'

'That's what I intend to find out. I'll be in touch. Just keep her safe.'

She ran back to the car, drove back to the house and let herself in, to find Matt sitting on the stairs, looking confused.

'What are you doing?' he asked.

Fear clawed at her.

'N-nothing.'

'So where have you been? Where's Emily? Sarah, what's wrong?' He stumbled down the last step and lurched towards her, then sagged against the wall, clutching his head.

She stepped back hastily. She must have been mad, coming back here for answers. Let the police find them.

'I—I have to go,' she stammered, fumbling the door catch, but suddenly he was there, holding the door shut, leaning on her.

He was burning up, but he was still stronger than she was. 'Where's Emily?' he repeated.

'Safe! Now let me go!'

He looked at her steadily for a moment, then closed his eyes. 'You know,' he said flatly. 'The video.' He swore under his breath and stabbed his hands through his hair. 'I didn't want you to find out this way—'

'What do you want with us?' Sarah asked frantically. Stay calm, she told herself. Try and reason with him. He might be mad. 'Matt, what's it all about? Whatever it is, can't we be reasonable? Please, don't hurt Emily—'

'Hurt Emily? Why on earth should I hurt Emily?' he said patiently. 'She's my niece, Sarah. Brad's my half-brother.'

She gaped at him. 'Your what?'

'My half-brother. We had the same mother.'

She felt the strength drain out of her. She leaned

against the door and stared at him, looking for answers to questions she'd hardly begun to formulate.

'So—why—?'

'Come and sit down. I'll explain.'

Explain? How?

She followed him into the sitting room. He sprawled in a chair, his face chalk white, looking awful. He also looked past harming anyone. She perched on a chair opposite, poised for flight, and waited.

'Brad and Helen are dead, Sarah,' he said heavily. 'They were killed in a car smash nearly two years ago in Germany.'

'Dead?' Brad and Helen, dead? Her hand flew up to her mouth, holding in the cry of anguish. 'Oh, no,' she moaned.

'I'm sorry. The police called me late one night. I flew to Germany and picked up Emily. We flew back on the plane with their bodies, and they were buried in Canada. Their bits and pieces were packed and sent on later— that's where the videos came from. According to the terms of their will, Emily came to live with me and Selina, and within two months Selina had walked out. She said she'd never planned to have a child, and she sure as hell wasn't having anybody else's.'

'So you thought you'd dump her on me,' Sarah said, light dawning. Brad and Helen, dead. Oh, my poor friends. My poor baby.

Tears welled in her eyes. 'I'll have her, of course,' she told him. 'We just need to sort out the legal side.'

'But that's not a problem. You're her mother, I've adopted her—there won't be a problem once we're married—'

'Married? *Married?* Are you crazy? You don't really think I'll marry you, do you? Now? After you've lied to me?'

'I haven't lied—'

'What? Are you quite mad? You told me you and Emily's mother were divorced.'

'No, I told you *my wife* and I were divorced.'

'Well, that's a lie by implication—and anyway, you told me she didn't want to be a mother—'

'She didn't. That's why she left us.'

'And why you decided to come over here and find me, so you could leave Emily with me and dump her, abdicating your responsibility!'

He shook his head slightly, wincing with pain. 'No, I would never abdicate my responsibility to Emily. That's why I adopted her. I came over here to find you because I felt very strongly that you and Emily deserved the chance to get to know each other.'

'So why not just tell me?'

He closed his eyes. 'I had my reasons.'

'Which were?'

He shrugged. 'The money, for a start.'

She stared at him. 'Money? What money?'

'The money Brad and Helen sent you when Emily was a month old.'

She couldn't see the relevance. 'That money. What about it?'

'It was paid into your personal account.'

'So?'

His eyes flew open. 'It's illegal to sell babies,' he pointed out harshly. 'I had to find out if you were a heartless mercenary.'

'Mercenary?' She felt sick. 'You thought I kept the money? You thought it was for me?'

'Wasn't it?'

He really believed it. She felt sicker.

'No, it wasn't!'

'So why didn't you mention it?'

'Mention it? Why should I mention it? It was none of your business. Brad and Helen insisted on sending me something that I could give to a charity of my choice, and that's exactly what I did. I paid it to a charity— several charities, actually. A SIDS charity that I support, the bereavement association, Cruse, the RNLI, the Samaritans—all sorts of places.'

'Not according to my investigator.'

'Your *what*!'

'Investigator. According to him, it remained in your account.'

Fury gripped her. 'My husband and children were killed that month, Matt,' she told him savagely. 'I wasn't really worrying about where to give the money at that point, but I can assure you I did give it, all of it, to various charities about six months later.'

'So you say. Then a few weeks ago you went out on the scrounge—'

'What? I was tin-shaking—collecting for the SIDS charity!' She stood up and marched over to the window, glaring out into the night. 'I suppose you thought I was begging—or, worse still, engaging in prostitution!'

'Don't be ridiculous.'

She snorted. 'Don't call me ridiculous. You're the one being ridiculous. Why on earth should I be out on the scrounge? I earn a living, I own my house—why would I need more?'

'I don't know—you tell me.'

'You're being absurd.'

'So how do you explain my rent?'

'Your rent?'

'Yes, my rent. I pay you a substantial amount to live here—I wondered at first if you were in financial difficulties, or if you might have a habit.'

She was dumbfounded. 'A habit? You think I'm on drugs?'

He shrugged. 'Stranger things have happened. You have a demanding job, it was possible. I don't now, of course.'

'Oh, how good of you. So I'm not allowed to charge you rent in case you think I'm a junkie, is that it?' she said waspishly.

'Yes, of course you are, but it was hardly the nominal sum a friend might set.'

'Nor did I keep it, if you must know. It also went to SIDS charities, for monitors. I don't have an extravagant lifestyle. I don't need a lot of money. It's enough to have a roof over my head, clothes to wear, a job where I can be of use and my health. Nothing else matters any more. Why do I need money?'

He closed his eyes. 'I'm sorry. I had to check you out, for Emily's sake, because she comes with a big inheritance, and it's hers.'

'Of course it's hers!' Sarah fumed, furious that he could have judged her like this, furious that she could have misjudged him at the same time.

She sat down again with a plop at the end of the sofa and stared at him, a sudden hideous thought dawning on her.

'Just tell me something. When, if ever, did you intend to tell me?'

He sighed. 'On Sunday, but your parents came round and Emily was sick. Since then everything's gone to hell.'

It certainly had. She felt shaky and confused and very, very frightened. 'If I hadn't said yes to your proposal, what did you intend to do, Matt?' she asked, suddenly panic-stricken. 'Were you just going to take Emily back to Canada with you, so I'd never see her again?'

'Of course not,' he said shortly, but it was easy to say.

'You were,' she accused. 'You were just going to take her.'

'No. I was going to take the job Jack offered me if you said yes, and look for another one nearby if he said no, because watching you and Emily together has made me sure beyond any shred of doubt that you belong together—but I wasn't sure if you were ready for that.'

She frowned. 'Not ready? But why ever not?'

He shrugged. 'You've avoided her on occasions. You won't put her to bed or kiss her goodnight if I'm here to do it—'

'So we didn't both get too attached! I could feel the bond strengthening every day—and I was dreading you taking her back to Canada.'

He gave her a level look. 'I would have left her with you, you know—if you'd wanted that, and she did too. I would have left her here with you and moved away—maybe even back to Canada, if she didn't need me.'

She snorted. 'I thought you said you loved her.'

'I do love her!' he snarled. 'Of course I love her—I adopted her! Why would I do that if I planned to palm her off on you and leg it?'

Could she believe him? Maybe, at some point in the future, but for now she was too hurt and confused to trust anyone.

Matt was standing up. 'Look, Sarah, I'm really not up to this right now,' he said wearily. 'I feel like hell and I just need to go to bed. Can we talk tomorrow?'

She hugged herself for comfort. 'If we must. I suppose there are things to decide. Here...'

She reached inside the neck of her uniform and pulled out a chain, then took the ring off it and handed it to him. 'This is yours. Keep it. I never want to see it again.'

Something like pain flickered in his eyes, and he turned and went out slowly, leaning on the wall.

'Take some aspirin,' she called after him.

He turned in the doorway. 'Sure—how many? Fifty? A hundred? How many would you like me to take, Sarah?'

'Two—and don't be silly.'

'Oh, I wasn't. Right now, if it wasn't for Emily, I really couldn't give a damn if I lived or died. It seems I'm not the only one.'

And with that he turned on his heel and left her alone with her thoughts.

She rang Ryan and said she'd explain the next day, but to please keep Emily and send her to school the next morning.

'In her nightdress?'

'Oh, hell.'

'We'll find her something of Evie's. Sarah, what's going on?' he asked gently.

She shook her head. 'Ryan, I can't— Don't ask me now. I don't think I'll be in tomorrow. I have too much to think about. Can you tell them?'

'Sure. You take as long as you need.' There was a pause, and he added, 'Sarah, you are safe, aren't you? Matt hasn't done anything to you?'

She gave a hollow laugh. 'Not in the way you mean. No, I'm safe. I'll talk to you tomorrow, Ryan. Thanks.'

She sat down in front of the television again and watched the video once more, unable to believe that Helen and Brad were dead. They looked so well, and yet Matt said they'd died just weeks afterwards.

Scalding tears splashed over her cheeks. Poor Emily. How had she coped with losing them? They'd loved her so much, been so thrilled with her. Their love showed in the video—in their voices and Helen's laughing face—and Emily must have been bereft without the comfort of their love.

But she would have love now. Sarah would make sure of it. What a strange twist of fate—to give her back the child she'd longed for so desperately, the child she'd mourned almost as much as the boys.

But she knew, if she could influence things, she'd turn the clock back so that Helen and Brad didn't die because she'd seen the sorrow on Emily's face when she'd talked about her mother, and she knew just what that loss had done to her little girl.

However, she couldn't, and she had a duty and responsibility now to make sure that Emily was just as happy as she could possibly be, and as safe and secure and wanted as Toby and James had been.

Even if she would never know that Sarah, and not Helen, was her mother...

She woke up the next morning, feeling dreadful. Her throat hurt, her eyes were gritty, her chest was agonising and she wanted to die. Of all the lousy timing, she thought, and crept downstairs for some aspirin. It stayed down, mercifully, and she felt a little better, but she couldn't eat, and she couldn't face the cup of tea she'd made, so she went back to bed with a glass of iced water and crawled under the covers.

Matt came in a while later and stood at the end of the bed.

'Have you got it?'

She nodded. 'I'm all right—leave me alone.'

He went, after a moment, but he was in the house all day, pottering around and keeping an eye on her. She got steadily worse, and by the end of the day she was forced to accept his help.

He washed her down, wiping her body with a warm,

damp flannel to bring her temperature down, changing her nightshirt—doing all the intimate things a lover would do, only he wasn't her lover, not now, not any more.

She thanked him ungraciously and sank back against the fresh, cool pillows. He'd changed the sheets for her, even though he still looked rough, and then he went round to Ryan's to talk to them.

She was sick again while he was out, and he came back to find her lying on the floor in her room, crying weakly with frustration because she couldn't make it back to bed.

He lifted her easily in his arms and laid her down gently, then sat on the side of the bed. 'I've talked to Ryan and Ginny, and told them what's going on. They're going to keep Em for now—she's better there until we've sorted this out. She thinks it's because we've both got flu, but the first thing we have to do is get you well. I'm going to bring you some aspirin—'

'No,' she moaned, and turned her head away.

'It will help. I've made up some electrolyte—'

'No-o.'

'Baby. I'll see you in a minute.'

He came back with the hideous mixtures and coaxed them down her throat, then held her head while she lost them again some time later.

'Why are you doing this for me?' she asked miserably. 'Why don't you just leave me alone?'

'Because I love you,' he said quietly. 'Now sip this.'

She met his eyes. 'I hate you for what you've done— you know that, don't you?'

Pain clouded his eyes. 'Yes, I know that. I'm sorry. I had no choice.'

'There's always a choice. You could have sent me a solicitor's letter.'

'No. It wasn't a job for a solicitor.'

She laughed unevenly. 'No. A solicitor wouldn't have been able to seduce me in quite the same way—Matt, go away.'

He went without a word, and left her wallowing in misery.

They didn't speak about it again that day, but next morning Matt came into her room with a drink of honey and lemon. 'Try this, it's got aspirin in. You might be able to keep it down and then you should feel better.'

He hesitated. 'Listen, downstairs by the television I've put a stack of video tapes of Emily right from birth through to that last one that you've seen. I thought you might like to look at them. There's also a file of paperwork you might want to go through when you feel a bit better, but some of it might need explaining. I'm off to work now. I'll see you later.'

'Matt?' She reached for him to stop him going, suddenly worried. 'Matt, don't tell anyone at work about this.'

He nodded slowly. 'OK. You know Ryan knows?'

'But he won't tell anyone.'

'No, of course he won't. Don't worry, Sarah, it'll be OK.'

Would it? She waited for the front door to close behind him, then pulled on her old jogging suit for warmth and crept downstairs, feeling like death warmed up. The honey and lemon had stayed down, amazingly, but she didn't want to push her luck. She'd have something else later.

For now, though, she wanted to look at the videos of her child.

Matt was gutted. Things had been going so well, and all of a sudden it had all backfired and she hated him. He

felt sick still, weak and shaky and not really well enough
to come back to work, but he wanted to give Sarah a
chance to look through the videos on her own.

Poor little Em had been confused and a bit clingy last
night, as if she'd realised there was more to it than just
flu. After all, *she'd* had flu and there hadn't been any
fuss. Poor love. He'd hugged her—hell, he'd been a bit
clingy himself, but who could blame him? Who was she
going to live with, if he couldn't sort this thing out with
Sarah?

The thought of losing her made him cold inside. He
couldn't lose her—or Sarah. He'd have to sort it out.

But how?

Let her get better, he thought. Let her get over the
initial shock, look at the videos, read through the cor-
respondence with the solicitor and the investigator. Let
her see how much thought and planning has gone into
this, to make sure that it runs smoothly for both of them
and that her daughter is protected. Let her come to terms
with it. Just be patient. He gave a short laugh. Patience
wasn't his strong suit.

'What's funny?' Patrick asked, coming up behind
him.

'Nothing. What's happening?'

'Nothing much. You look grim. Where's Sarah? Still
sick?'

He nodded. 'Yes—it's—ah—short but nasty. She'll
be up and about soon.'

Patrick seemed to accept that. Not that there was any
reason why he shouldn't because half the department
had been stricken with the bug since Evie had given it
to Ryan.

Ryan was back, and towed Matt into the staffroom in
a quiet moment. 'Are you OK?'

'I'm fine—well, no, I'm not fine, that's a lie, but I'll live. How's Em this morning?'

'Worried. She thinks Sarah's very sick.'

Matt shook his head. 'She's better now, a bit. She was bad last night.'

Ryan chased a dribble of water on the worktop with his finger. 'Will you tell her Sarah's her mother?'

'I don't know. I think Sarah should tell her, in her own time, but for now Sarah can't seem to get past the fact that I wasn't upfront at the beginning.'

'So why weren't you?'

'Because I fell for her, Ryan, like a ton of bricks, and I wanted to give us a chance. I wanted to know if she wanted me, or just Emily. Once she knew who Em was, that chance was gone.'

'And you thought you could tell her after you proposed and it would all be hunky-dory?'

He smiled crookedly. 'That's the one.'

Ryan put an arm round his shoulders. 'Oh, Matt. The trouble with Sarah is that everything's been snatched away from her. She daren't trust anything or take it for granted. I couldn't believe how happy she was when things between you were going well.'

He snorted. 'Well, things aren't going well now, Ryan, I can assure you.'

'I hate to break up the party,' Jack said drily from the doorway, 'but there's a queue out here and two ambulances on the way in. I don't suppose either of you would like to do some work today?'

For a while it was bedlam. Matt would have enjoyed the pressure under normal circumstances, but as it was he felt dreadful and he got shunted off the Resus case and sidelined into dealing with the 'Treat and Streets'.

That suited him. Short consultations, minor injuries, nothing drastic—or if there was, he missed it. He didn't think so. He wasn't that far gone, but he wasn't an asset to the department as far as his speed went.

He stared at a Colles' fracture for a full minute, turning it this way and that, before he could make his mind focus on it.

'Do you think it's broken?' the elderly lady said in the end, tentatively nudging him towards a diagnosis.

'Oh. Um, yes, I'm afraid it is broken. It's a Colles' fracture—see, it's bent like a fork, with your wrist curved up? We'll take a picture just to make sure there's nothing untoward, then we can sort it out for you and get a plaster on it.'

It took ages, of course—Colles' fractures always did. He reduced it under local anaesthetic to save the trauma of a general. That was always a palaver because the veins had to be emptied, the circulation cut off by a blood pressure cuff, the anaesthetic introduced into a vein and allowed to infiltrate the tissues and numb them completely. Then after it was reduced and re-X-rayed, the cuff was removed and the patient monitored to make sure the local anaesthetic now spreading round the system didn't have an adverse effect.

Fortunately she was fine, and he sent her off to lie down in the recovery area with her husband and wait for a while, before going home.

It was to be an orthopaedics day, he discovered. While they were waiting for the Colles' fracture lady's anaesthetic to wear off, a very upset young woman brought in a child of three who was holding his arm awkwardly. His elbow was slightly bent, his arm turned in and held very stiffly, and he was snivelling a bit.

'Matthew?'

The boy nodded and sniffed, reaching for his mother's hand.

'Well, isn't that funny? That's my name too. So,

Matthew, what happened to you?' he asked, squatting to the child's level.

'He ran off the kerb and I grabbed him, and now his arm hurts. I thought he was going to be hit by a car, and instead I've hurt him!'

'Hush, it's all right,' he said, smiling up at the young woman. 'It often happens. Is he your little boy?'

She nodded. 'Yes.'

'OK, Matthew, let's take your jumper off very, very carefully and see if we can have a look at this.'

They sat him on the bed and peeled the jumper off carefully, good arm first, then head. Matt touched the end of his radius gently but firmly.

'Ow!'

'Right. This looks very straightforward. Matthew, what I'm going to do is turn your arm slowly in and out, and push down a little bit, and then it will go click, just like this.' He clicked one of his finger joints so that the boy could see it wouldn't hurt, and then smiled. 'OK?'

He nodded doubtfully. Matt looked at the mother. 'Could you put your arm round his shoulder and hold his other hand to help him? And, Matthew, will you be very brave for me?'

The little boy nodded again, still doubtful, and Matt sent up a quick prayer for an easy reduction. Usually it was a piece of cake, but today, of course, it would probably be difficult.

Nope. It went straight back, and Matt gave an inward sigh of relief and beamed at them both. 'Now, how does that feel?'

The little boy straightened his arm, wriggled it about and laughed. 'It doesn't hurt any more,' he said with a delighted grin.

'Good. Excellent. Now, remember, don't go running out into the road without your mummy, OK?'

He nodded, and Matt sent them off, two satisfied customers, and went back to his Colles' lady.

The secretary came and found him just as he was about to call his next patient. 'Your daughter's school phoned—she's very distressed about something and they can't get any sense out of her. Can you go?'

He looked round the crowded waiting room and sighed. 'Now?'

'They sounded quite worried.'

'I'll talk to her on the phone. I'll ring from the office.'

He went and found Ryan. 'Can I use your office?' he asked tightly.

'Sure—what's the problem?'

'Em—she's distressed. I knew this would happen.'

'Why don't you just go to her?'

'The waiting room's full—'

'We can cope. You aren't even officially here on our head count, you're just a bonus. For God's sake, go.'

He went, without any further encouragement.

Emily was in the secretary's office, sobbing hysterically on the woman's lap.

'Ah, sweetheart,' Matt murmured as he took her. Her arms fastened round his neck and she buried her face in his shoulder.

'I don't want Sarah to die,' she wept.

He squeezed her hard. 'Sarah's not going to die, darling. She's got the flu—the same flu you had. She'll be fine.'

She sniffed and lifted her head. 'Somebody said you could die with flu.'

'Not this sort,' he assured her firmly. 'Now, come on, I'll take you home to see her, all right?'

She nodded wetly into his collar, and he thanked the secretary and carried Emily out to the car. She was very quiet during the journey, and Matt kept an eye on her in the rear-view mirror, but she sat with her finger in her mouth, wiggling her wobbly tooth.

When they pulled up on the drive she had her seat belt off by the time he opened the car door. She ran up to the front door and reached up for the knob.

'Hang on, sprout, give me a moment.' He put his key in the lock and turned it, and Emily ran into the sitting room.

'Are you all right?' she was asking, and Matt followed her in to find her sitting on the sofa with Sarah, staring earnestly into her face.

'Of course I'm all right. I've just got flu.'

'I thought you were dying,' Emily said theatrically, and Sarah laughed and hugged her.

'No, darling, I'm not dying.'

'So why are you crying?'

Sarah sniffed. 'I'm not. It's the flu—it makes my eyes water.'

Matt held his hand out to Emily. 'Come on, sprout, let's go and get you a drink and find you a biscuit.'

He met Sarah's eyes over her head, and they were full of emotion.

'I need to talk to you,' she said.

He nodded. 'OK. Later. How about a drink?'

'If I must.'

'You must. Tea?'

She grimaced. 'Just weak, not too much milk.'

They came back in a few moments later and Matt was pleased to see Sarah was a bit more composed. He didn't dare to hope that everything was all right, but she smiled at him as if she didn't hate his guts, and a little flicker of optimism fanned into life.

Maybe—just maybe it was all going to be all right...

CHAPTER TEN

'ARE you watching my videos?' Emily asked, snuggling up beside Sarah.

Sarah let herself hold the child close because they both needed the contact, and nodded. 'Yes, I have been.' In between reading that file of Matt's.

'Can we watch them again? I haven't seen them for ages.'

'OK.'

Matt knelt on the floor and plugged the first one in, then came and crouched in front of them. 'Are you guys OK together if I go back to work?'

'Yes, we're fine,' she told him, and reached for his hand, squeezing it. 'Don't worry.'

His eyes searched hers. He looked puzzled and hopeful and confused. Never mind, she'd talk to him later.

'You won't do anything rash?' he said cautiously.

'No, of course not.'

He still hesitated, but Emily turned her face up to him and smiled. 'You go, Daddy—I can look after Sarah.'

He went, and Sarah hugged Emily—her daughter— and smiled at her. 'All right now, little one?'

She nodded. 'I was just worried about you. I didn't want you to die—not as well as my mummy and daddy.'

'Oh, sweetheart.'

She had to stop herself from crushing the child.

They watched all the videos, with Emily telling her what she could remember from each one, and Sarah absorbed the details of her daughter's life like a sponge.

She'd already watched most of them through once,

but it was only two o'clock and there were a few still to go.

And there in the corner was the file on her that Matt had carefully kept since he'd begun his search for her over a year ago. It explained so much, but there was more she wanted to ask him about. She'd have to wait. He'd be home at six or so.

Time dragged. It was eight o'clock before Emily was in bed asleep, and by then Matt was so tense Sarah thought if she hit him he'd shatter.

He came running downstairs and came to a halt in the kitchen doorway. She turned and smiled cautiously. 'Asleep?'

'I think so, pretty much.'

She handed him a cup of tea and picked hers up. 'Shall we go and sit down?'

He followed her in a silence fraught with suspense, and as she curled up in a chair he perched on the edge of the sofa, waiting.

'I owe you an apology,' she began. 'I read your file on me—it seems I misjudged you. You're quite right, you had to make sure everything was OK, before introducing me to Emily, but I overreacted. It was just such a shock.'

'I'm sure. I didn't want to do it like that, and the last thing I wanted was for you to find out that way,' he said. 'I wanted to tell you up front, as soon as I was happy that everything was as it seemed, but by then I'd fallen in love with you.' He looked down at his hands. 'I didn't mean to, and I certainly didn't mean to sleep with you.'

'You can't tell me that was spontaneous,' she came back instantly. 'That was planned down to the last carrot stick and candle.'

He lifted his head a little and gave her a wry, caught-in-the-cookie-jar grin. 'OK. It was a little planned, but only from the night before. It was right for us at the time, and I'm not made of stone. I needed you, you needed me—it was right. There hasn't been anyone since Selina walked out on me. I had Emily to consider, and sex came a long way down the list of priorities in those early days.

'Then the PI started sending me photos of you, and a video with some footage of you on it shot in the A and E department for a news report, and suddenly I couldn't see anybody else. When I met you and found you were even lovelier than I'd thought, I was lost.'

'What a lot of old flannel.' She laughed.

Matt shook his head, a smile lurking round his eyes. 'It isn't. I'd already fallen in love with your eyes on the video. When they looked at me in that special way, I was sunk.'

'So sunk that you quizzed me about all the painful and tragic things that had happened to me over the past few years?'

He exhaled harshly. 'That was difficult for me.'

'Difficult for *you*?'

'Yes, difficult for me. I knew what it would do to you—'

'So why do it? I'm still angry about that, Matt. You made me tell you all the gory details, about how they died and how I coped, and all the time it was there in that file—'

'Not all,' he said quietly. 'The bald facts, yes, but not your reaction. Not your viewpoint, your emotions—I had the feeling you needed to talk about it. I also had the feeling you didn't do that very often, and who better than me? I already knew all the details, so I wasn't going to put my foot in it—and, believe it or not, I cared.'

She made a rude noise. 'You hardly knew me. How could you possibly care?'

'You were Emily's mother,' he said simply. 'You're very alike. The moment I met you I felt as if I'd known you and worked with you for years.'

He pulled a face. 'I meant to stay away from you until I'd told you about Emily, but then I thought, you'd lost so much, of course you'd want her, and I wouldn't know if you wanted me for myself or just for Emily because it was tidy. And I needed to know that. Selina wanted me for what I had to offer—a good salary, a certain standing in the community—I didn't want to be wanted again for the wrong reasons.'

'And you thought if you told me who Emily really was, I wouldn't be able to separate the two of you?' she said, understanding now quite clearly the dilemma he'd faced.

'Would you have been able to, in my shoes?'

She shook her head. 'No. I still wish you'd told me, but you're right—from your point of view it was the right thing to do. It doesn't help me, though, because I don't know if you want me because you love me or just because it's tidy and I'm willing and—'

'Sarah! I wouldn't marry you because it was tidy!'

'Not even for Emily's sake?' she asked gently.

He sighed and ran his hands over his face. 'No, I don't think so, not even for Emily's sake. We'd work something out. Divorced couples work something out. It wouldn't be so very different. We could live near each other and share custody.'

'You said you'd give her up if necessary.'

His head snapped up, his eyes wary and watchful. 'Is that what you want?' he asked tautly.

She shook her head, and some of the tension went out

of his shoulders. 'So what do you want?' he asked and
then waited, motionless, for her reply.

'I want us to get married,' she told him. 'I've calmed
down now and thought about it, and it's the best thing
for all of us.'

'And do you trust me now, absolutely?'

She looked deep into his eyes and saw no trace of the
teasing, boyish humour that had lurked in their grey
depths just a few minutes ago. Instead, she saw a man
of honour and integrity—a man worth loving. A man
she could trust?

'I want to,' she said honestly. 'I want to, but—I don't
know. It's a leap of faith, and I'm not very good at that.'

'Can't you try?'

'It's not easy for me to trust,' she said slowly. 'I've
lost so much. This is all so tidy—why would fate work
like that? Matt, I work in A and E, I know about fate.
It's a vindictive bitch. When things go right, I don't trust
it.'

'Sometimes you just have to.'

'I've read all the letters,' she told him. 'The warning
from the solicitor that I might fight you for Emily and
you might lose—whatever happens, Matt, you do realise
I wouldn't ask that of you, don't you? I know how much
you love her. I love her too, and I wouldn't want anything else to hurt her. That's why I don't want to marry
you unless you're doing it for me and not just to make
sure you don't lose her—because you won't lose her. I
wouldn't let that happen to either of you. I love you both
too much.'

'Would you say that again?' he said very carefully.

She took a steadying breath. 'I love you—'

He was across the room before she'd finished speaking. He scooped her up and sat down with her on his
lap, cradled against his chest.

'I thought I'd lost all chance of hearing you say that,' he murmured. 'Oh, Sarah, trust me—please? I'd never do anything to hurt you—or Emily either.'

'I'd rather we were just friends than married and later fell out,' she told him honestly. 'I couldn't bear to hurt her any more—or to lose her again.'

'You won't lose her, I promise. Whatever else might happen, you won't lose her, not now.'

Their eyes met. 'I never expected this to happen,' he went on. 'The most I'd hoped for was a simple agreement from you to share custody. At the least I thought you might either not be interested, or fight me for her. I never dreamed we might end up together.'

He cupped her cheek. 'I don't trust fate either, darling. I never have. It's never done me any favours before, except maybe giving me Emily and freeing me from Selina. Maybe it's our time for things to go right.'

Her mind was in turmoil. 'I don't believe in happy ever after,' she said sadly. 'I don't think you do, either, and yet you told the solicitor that you understood the risk of coming to find me. You said if you lost her so be it because we deserved the chance to get to know each other. That was a very brave thing to do.'

'It wasn't brave at all. I was scared to death, but I had no choice. I couldn't have lived with myself if I hadn't done it—especially after I found out that you'd lost Rob and the boys. You had so little left, and it was in my power to give you so much. How could I not do that?'

She chewed her lip thoughtfully. 'I still wish you hadn't had me investigated.'

He heaved a sigh. 'I had to get a PI to trace you. You'd moved, there was no way of knowing where to. I didn't have the time or the skills to come over here and do it myself. Anyway, I had to be careful for Emily's sake, but I hated doing it. If it had just been me

I would have used my judgement, but I owed it to Emily to make sure nothing else could go wrong with her world. I didn't want to spy on you. I just needed to know that Emily would be safe with you.'

'You do know she is?'

He nodded. 'I do now.'

She looked into his eyes. 'I want this to work so much,' she told him quietly.

'So marry me,' he pressed. 'I vow I'll spend the rest of my life proving that you did the right thing.'

She searched his face, and it was like an open book. There were no lies there, no secrets. Her heart felt suddenly light. Of course everything would be all right. He was the only one, after all, who had anything to lose. Of course she could trust him.

She laid her hand against his cheek, relishing the hard, stubbly jaw, and smiled. 'You'd better not let me down,' she said threateningly. 'I shall hold you to that promise.'

'Is that a yes?'

She nodded, and his eyes crinkled at the corners as he started to smile. 'Better marry you quick, then, before you change your mind.'

She chuckled and bent to kiss him, and Emily's little voice cut through the mist of happiness surrounding them.

'Does that mean you're going to be my new mummy?'

Sarah's head came up and she met Emily's thoughtful eyes. How much had she heard?

'Would you like that, darling?' she asked cautiously.

'Oh, yes.' Emily hesitated. 'I thought it would be nice if I could have my other mummy. Mummy told me about her, and said she'd loved me very much but she'd given me to her because my mummy couldn't have a baby. I'd like to see her, but she's got babies anyway so I don't 'spect she'd want me, and I know you do, so that's OK. I love you anyway.'

So many mummies, but one thing was clear—Helen had told Emily she wasn't her own child.

Sarah looked at Matt for help. 'Um...'

'I think this needs a group hug. Shall we go on the sofa?'

They moved, settling down with Emily between them, and with pounding hearts, they asked Emily what she knew.

'Mummy had a big scar,' she told them matter-of-factly, 'and it meant she couldn't have babies in her tummy any more, so when she and Daddy wanted me, they couldn't. Then another lady said she'd have me for them, and keep me in her tummy until I was born, then give me to my mummy and daddy—so, you see, I had two mummies.'

They nodded, and Sarah felt a huge lump rising in her throat. 'Um—Emily, did your mummy tell you about your other mummy?'

She shook her head. 'Not really. I think she said she was called Sarah, like you.'

Sarah swallowed and looked at Matt for help. He nodded, and she took a deep breath.

'Emily—I *am* your other mummy. It was me that had you. I gave you to your Mummy and Daddy.'

Emily looked at her in amazement. 'And we met you, just like that?' she said incredulously.

'Not quite just like that. That's why we're here,' Matt told her. 'We came to find Sarah, so you two could be together.'

She looked stunned, as well she might, Sarah thought. It was a lot to take in at thirty. At five and a half, it must be horrendously complicated.

'So you really are my proper mummy?' Emily said slowly.

'Helen was your proper mummy,' she corrected. 'I was your natural mother—I carried you inside me, and gave birth to you. You are my child.'

Emily wriggled round and knelt, facing her. 'So I can really call you Mummy, and you really are?'

Sarah gulped down the emotion and nodded. 'Yes, darling, you can, and I really am.'

She sat there for a moment more, then tipped her head on one side just as Helen used to do. 'Didn't you mind giving me away?' she asked.

'Oh, Emily, if you only knew how much...'

Tears welled in her eyes, and with a little cry Emily threw herself into Sarah's arms and hugged her tight. 'Never mind, Mummy, you've got me back now, and I'm never going to go away from you again!'

'I don't believe it! How can we have a major incident? It's the night before the wedding—how can this happen?'

Matt shrugged his shoulders. 'That's trauma for you.'

'No,' Sarah corrected bluntly, 'that's fate, interfering again. I told my mother not to buy a special outfit.'

'And you haven't?'

She tapped her nose and smiled. 'You'll just have to wait and see—if we're out of here on time.'

'We might be late, Sarah, but make your mind up to it—we're getting married tomorrow if we have to drag the chaplain down here to do it!'

'Good. What is it, anyway?' Sarah asked him. 'A pile-up?'

'No, an aircraft. It crashed somewhere just north-west of here—bellyflopped in a field. It's broken up and there are several burn victims, crush injuries, smoke inhalation, whiplash, multiple injuries—you name it. The burns and head injuries are going to Cambridge, and the rest are being divided up between the local hospitals.'

'How many?'

'Lots—we can expect fifteen or twenty in the first hour, apparently, others to follow. Two teams have gone up there and they're calling all the GPs out to help with the triage so they can prioritise.'

'We'll need to use the fracture clinic as an overflow waiting area for the walking wounded and relatives—it's got several offices that can be used for relatives. What about the dead?'

'They'll be brought here for identification and post-mortem. I gather most of them will be identified from dental records. The fire was pretty hot.'

'Great. So we've got some burns as well?'

'Most of them will go direct to Cambridge, but we may get some with burns and multiple injuries who need to be stabilised for transfer.'

She looked down at her watch and sighed. 'I'll ring Mum. She's got Emily anyway, but she ought to know I won't be coming back tonight.'

'It's unlucky to see the groom on your wedding day,' he reminded her. 'You'll have to keep out of my way.'

She chuckled. 'That's fine. I expect I'll be cross-eyed with exhaustion by the end of the night so I probably won't see you anyway. You'll just have to work with someone else.'

'Like hell. You stay close.'

They were too busy to notice. They were on the run for most of the night, checking vital signs, stabilising people in shock from blood loss, ordering X-rays, stitching and plastering and reassuring, taking details and trying to find out what had happened to relatives.

Counsellors were brought in to talk to relatives of the

dead and missing, and the whole process ran like clock-
work from the moment the doors burst open with the
first spate of casualties.

Jack put them in teams and they worked in the two
Resus rooms, each of which could take up to three patients at a time. Doctors from other parts of the hospital
were called in to work on the walking wounded, leaving
the treatment of critically injured and unstable patients
to the specialist A and E teams and any surgeons not
already occupied in Theatre.

Matt and Sarah worked together on some, separately
on others. They were together, about an hour after the
first casualties had arrived, working on one young man
who was arresting, when there was a ringing sound from
the bag of his clothing and effects.

It stopped them dead. 'Oh, Lord, it's a mobile phone,'
Sarah said after a few seconds. 'Who's calling him?'

'Get it,' Matt told her, thumping the man in the chest.
'Be vague.'

'Vague? What do I say—sorry, you just missed him?'
She rummaged for the phone, pressed what looked like
the on switch and held it to her ear. 'Hello?'

'Who is that? Where's Steve? What's going on?'

'My name is Sarah Cooper—I'm a nurse at the
Audley Memorial Hospital. Can I ask who you are?'

'Lucy—Lucy Laughlin. Where's Steve?'

'He's here, I believe. Is Steve the owner of the
phone?' Sarah asked.

'Yes, he's my husband— Oh, my God, what's happened to him? Has he crashed? Let me speak to him,
please.'

'Stand back,' Matt was saying, and Steve's body
arched and flopped as he was shocked.

'I'm sorry, he's not able to talk to you at the moment,'
Sarah said calmly. 'There's been an accident and we're

treating him at the moment. Can you give me a description?'

'Um—six foot, dark hair, glasses—he's twenty eight.'

'Any distinguishing marks?'

'Um...oh, a scar on his shin—he had a fracture three years ago.'

Sarah flipped back the blanket and looked at the patient's leg. Sure enough, a neat scar ran the length of one shin. 'Yes, it must be him. Can you give me his full name?'

'Stephen James Laughlin. Please, what's going on?'

Sarah watched the trace on the monitor pick up and recover, and let out a silent sigh of relief. 'Mrs Laughlin, are you able to come to the hospital? Your husband's plane had to make an emergency landing and several of the passengers have been injured. I'm afraid he's one of them. We'll be able to tell you more in a little while if you could come in.'

'Oh, dear God! Will he need to stay in?' the anxious woman asked. 'I'd better bring him something—what will he need? Is he badly hurt?'

'We'll find him something for now—you just come, nice and steadily. You'll be directed—tell them you're a relative of a patient under treatment. We'll hope to know more about his condition when you get here.'

She hung up and looked at Matt across Steve Laughlin's body. 'How is he?'

'Better than he was a minute ago. Wife?'

'Yes. She's coming in. Any idea what's wrong with him?'

'Spleen, I think. We're running in plasma expander through two large-bore needles, but we're scarcely holding him. We're going to run out of blood, too, if the new stocks don't arrive soon.'

They did, thankfully, and Steve Laughlin was sent up

to Theatre for emergency abdominal surgery. His wife
arrived shortly afterwards and signed the consent form,
but, as Sarah said, better late than never. He was one of
the lucky ones who'd needed to have a form signed.

Others were less lucky, and the bereavement counsellors were working flat out, dealing with shocked relatives.

The press were there in force, naturally, covering the
story of a small commercial plane which had crashed
and burst into flames, while carrying many local people
home from holidays or business trips. The phone never
stopped ringing, and Jack took a break to speak to the
press.

'Horrible job. People want to know—they need to
know, I suppose, but they just seem like vultures,' Sarah
said wearily. 'It seems so sordid.'

There was nobody unstable at that point, but there was
still a huge queue of those waiting to be seen with minor
injuries, and others still due to come in.

'Coffee,' Matt said firmly, stripping off his gloves and
gown as the patient they'd been working on was whisked
away to Theatre. 'Quick, before the next batch arrives.
We've got to relax and walk around, get the kinks out.'

He kneaded the muscles at the base of his neck wearily, and Sarah led him into the staffroom, put the kettle
on and sat him down. He leaned his head back against
her as she dug her fingers into his taut shoulders, and he
groaned.

'Pain or pleasure?' she asked with a laugh.

'Both. God, I needed that.' He stood up and took her
hands in his, drawing her into his arms. 'I need a hug
too.'

'It's after midnight. Our wedding day.'

'You'd better believe it.'

'Next time the chaplain appears, do you want to ask

him if he can switch the venue? The queues out there just aren't going to go away.'

'They'll go—and so will we. Don't worry, you don't get out of it.'

'I don't want to,' she told him firmly.

'Good. Made that coffee yet?'

'Oh, yes, with my other pair of hands.'

She made it, but they diluted it with cold water and drank it fast. Even then they were barely finished before a siren penetrated the pandemonium and the doors swished open again. As a trolley hit the ground and jolted slightly, the patient cried out in pain.

'This is Kate—she was trapped in her seat in the tail section. Injuries to lower right leg, otherwise seems stable. Back-board and collar just a precaution.'

'Thanks. Hello, Kate, I'm Sarah,' she called, bending over as they wheeled her quickly through to Resus. The poor girl cried out with every tiny bump, and Sarah could only guess at what she'd gone through in the ambulance. 'Soon have you more comfortable,' she promised.

They took the notes that were pinned to her blanket and scanned them.

'Right, she's had very little pain relief apart from Entonox, so let's give her 2.5 mg of morphine before we do anything else,' Matt said, glancing at the inflatable splint on her leg.

The blood loss was obvious, as was the strange angle of her lower leg.

'Let's get some pictures, please,' Matt said to the radiographer. She was already slotting loaded X-ray cassettes into place under the leg in question, and she glanced at Matt.

'Where else?'

'Spine and pelvis,' he said distractedly, trying to insert

another IV line into Kate's deflated veins. 'Sarah, open up that Haemaccel and squeeze it in, please.'

She unhooked the other IV line and pressed the bag, forcing the fluid into the patient faster before the circulation collapsed.

'Stand back,' the radiographer said, and they all moved out of line for a moment and then carried on.

Matt was looking at Kate's knees. Notwithstanding the funny angle of her lower leg, her right leg seemed to be turned out further than the left.

'Pelvis?'

He nodded. 'Could be. Right, I've got that other line in at last. Let's get this blood off for cross-matching immediately, and we'd better start her with O-neg.'

He deflated the splint, lifted aside the sterile dressing and winced. The skin over the whole of her lower leg had been peeled back like a banana, cutting off the blood supply to the rest of the skin, effectively killing the limb.

'Oh, dear,' Sarah said softly.

'Mmm. Always the pretty ones,' Matt said heavily. 'Right, let's get orthopaedics down here fast to sort this one out.'

The radiographer bustled back in with the plates and snapped them up into the light box. 'Here you go—nasty mess.'

It was. The patient's tibia was shattered so badly that she would probably have needed an amputation anyway, regardless of the soft tissue injury that had made it inevitable.

Her pelvis, as Matt had spotted, was broken in two places around the front and back, and the femur had been driven up into the socket, fracturing the acetabulum.

'She's going to hurt,' Matt murmured.

The door opened and one of the volunteers stuck her

head round. 'I'm looking for a Kate Lucas—she was trapped?'

'This young woman's Kate.'

'Her fiancé wants to know if she's all right, and if he can see her.'

They exchanged glances. 'She'll need surgery—can he sign for her?'

'He's not strictly next of kin,' Sarah reminded him.

'And this isn't strictly routine. See if he knows where her parents can be contacted—in fact, tell him the surgeon will come and talk to him.'

The volunteer nodded and vanished. 'I don't know when a surgeon will be able to talk to him—they're all busy,' Sarah reminded Matt. 'We'll just have to send her up when she's stable.'

'In which case, I'll go and talk to him now. I do love this job sometimes,' he murmured. 'I feel like a regular Santa Claus. "I've got a present for you—your fiancée's leg." Wow.'

He went, stripping off his gloves and throwing them dispiritedly into the bin. You win some, you lose some, Sarah thought, and then there are the ones you aren't sure have been won or lost.

Tricky.

It was five o'clock before they finally went off duty, twenty-one hours after the start of their shift and six hours before their wedding. They were exhausted, but the adrenaline which had kept them going was still circulating.

They went home to bed, and hesitated on the landing. They'd showered, had a cup of tea in the kitchen and gone back up just as dawn was breaking. In the thin light Sarah met Matt's eyes and saw a need that echoed her own.

'I ought to make you wait until tonight,' she said with a smile.

His voice was husky. 'I'll wait.'

'I don't want you to.' She went into his arms. 'I've missed you. It's been so long. Make love to me, Matt.'

His mouth came down hungrily. 'Oh, Sarah, I've missed you, too. That one night just wasn't enough. I don't think a lifetime will be enough.' Then he raised his head and swore softly.

'What is it?'

'No condoms,' he said succinctly. 'I was going to buy them this morning—we finished the last lot and I didn't get any for Valentine's Day because Emily was staying at home.' He released her and stepped back, his face taut. 'Hell. Sarah, go to bed.'

She moved towards him, not willing to let him go. 'I don't mind if you don't.'

He stared at her in the dim light. 'You might get pregnant.'

She smiled. 'Yes, I might. Actually it's quite likely at the moment.'

He swallowed hard, then took a deep breath. 'We've never actually discussed this.'

She hesitated. 'Don't you want a child?' she whispered. Oh, Lord, please, no, I want his child—

'Sarah, of course I want a child, more than you could imagine, but you've been through so much—'

'Oh, Matt! I love babies. I'm good at babies—and I want to have yours. Anyway, Emily's ordered one.'

He gave a strangled laugh. 'What?'

'Emily—she's put in her order for a little brother or sister for Christmas.'

He smiled slowly. 'Then we haven't got a minute to waste, have we?' He drew her back into his arms and kissed her lingeringly. 'Your room or mine?'

'Ours,' she said, and led him into the room she had occupied alone ever since she'd moved there. 'The bed's bigger, and there's such a lot of you.'

He grinned wickedly. 'You complaining?'

'Absolutely not. Come here.'

He growled softly and chased her across the room, catching her easily. After all, she didn't want to make it too difficult...

They didn't sleep at all. They made love tenderly, without haste, without self-consciousness, and then got up and showered again and dressed for the wedding.

Well, Matt did. Sarah put on her make-up and old jogging suit and he drove her to her parents'.

Then she shooed him away. 'You go—I'll see you at the hospital,' she told him.

He kissed her once more. 'I love you,' he said soberly. 'You do believe me, don't you?'

She smiled at him and hugged him. 'Yes, darling, I believe you. I love you, too. Now go, or I'll be late.'

She waved him off, then ran upstairs to her old bedroom followed by her mother.

'He's so good-looking in that dark suit and white shirt there should be a law against it,' her mother said with a smile. 'Happy?'

'Ecstatic.'

'Of course, he's not supposed to see you on your wedding day till you get to the church,' she chided.

Sarah laughed, so happy she could burst. 'There's no way seeing him could bring me bad luck,' she told her mother. 'Now, quick, help me get dressed.'

She pulled off her jogging suit and her mother gasped. 'Darling, whatever's happened to you? You've got sunburn!'

Sarah looked down and saw a faint red rash over her breasts and abdomen.

She blushed. 'Whisker-burn,' she corrected ruefully.

Her mother's hand flew up to her face and she gave a surprised laugh. 'Oh, Sarah! I know he's irresistible, but...'

Sarah laughed. 'Absolutely—and, anyway, we were working on a grandchild for you.'

'Conceived out of wedlock?'

But her mother's eyes were sparkling, and Sarah hugged her. 'Only just,' she pointed out, and dived into her dress. 'Do me up before Emily comes in and wants to know how I got sunburn in March.'

The zip slid quietly home and Sarah looked in the mirror. 'Is it OK? I wanted a long white dress, because of Emily and because I wanted it to be a real wedding, but I had a frilly one with Rob and I thought something simple—'

'Darling, it looks perfect.' Her mother tugged the skirt straight and stood back, admiring the absolute simplicity of the soft silk dress. It had a fine chiffon top and sleeves over a fitted chemise, and it was demure and yet tantalising. 'He'll probably choke when he sees you.'

Sarah laughed. 'I hope not. I'm not doing CPR on my wedding day—not even for him!'

Her mother hugged her gently. 'I'll miss you while you're in Canada.'

'It's only a month. We have to pack up all Matt's things and put his house on the market, and Emily needs to say goodbye to her old friends, then we'll be back for good.'

'With all my grandchildren.'

Sarah grinned. 'You bet.'

They made it to the hospital chapel in time, but only just. Matt was there, standing tall at the end of the aisle with Ryan beside him, and Ginny had Evie and Gus all dressed up and ready to join Emily as Sarah's attendants.

Ginny hugged her. 'Oh, Sarah, you look ravishing.'
She grinned. 'How appropriate!'

Ginny laughed, lined up the little ones and waved to the organist.

Matt was good, Sarah thought as she sailed down the aisle on her father's arm. He didn't turn round until right at the last moment, and when he did his response was all she could have asked for.

He didn't choke, exactly, but his eyes tracked to the shadow of her cleavage and then up to her eyes, and a promise danced in their blue-grey depths.

She took her place beside him, he took her hand, and the ceremony began.

It took her back—to another church, another wedding. It was funny how she could say the same words to another man and mean them just as sincerely, she thought.

She'd loved Rob very dearly, and would never have wanted him to die, but he had, and now Matt was here, and she could almost feel Rob and the boys with her, wishing them joy.

'I now pronounce you man and wife,' the chaplain said, smiling broadly.

Matt turned to her and looked down into her eyes. His thumb brushed her cheek, wiping away the tear. 'Are you OK?' he asked softly.

'Yes. Yes, I'm fine. I love you.'

'I love you, too,' he breathed against her lips, and kissed her.

And the ragamuffin crew from A and E, hard-nosed cynics to a man, sniffed and blinked in unison...

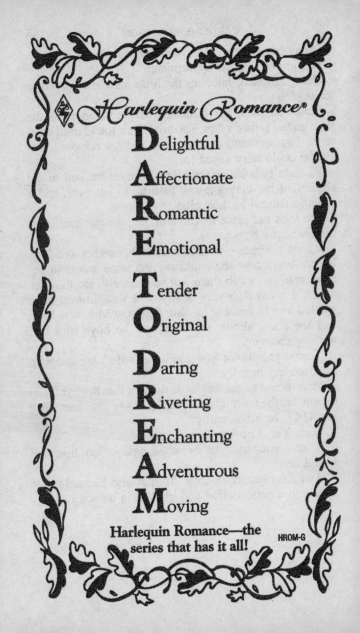

Harlequin Romance®

Delightful
Affectionate
Romantic
Emotional

Tender
Original

Daring
Riveting
Enchanting
Adventurous
Moving

Harlequin Romance—the
series that has it all!

HROM-G

HARLEQUIN ◆ PRESENTS®

HARLEQUIN PRESENTS
men you won't be able to resist
falling in love with...

HARLEQUIN PRESENTS
women who have feelings
just like your own...

HARLEQUIN PRESENTS
powerful passion in
exotic international settings...

HARLEQUIN PRESENTS
intense, dramatic stories that will keep you
turning to the very last page...

HARLEQUIN PRESENTS
The world's bestselling romance series!

PRES-G

Harlequin® Historical

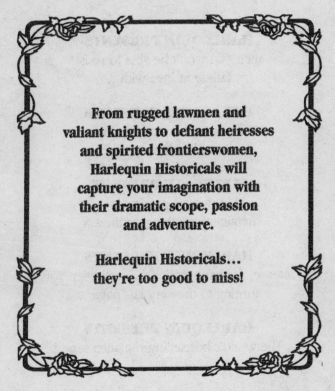

From rugged lawmen and
valiant knights to defiant heiresses
and spirited frontierswomen,
Harlequin Historicals will
capture your imagination with
their dramatic scope, passion
and adventure.

Harlequin Historicals…
they're too good to miss!

HHGENR

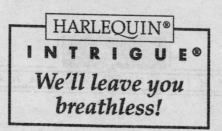

HARLEQUIN®

I N T R I G U E®

We'll leave you breathless!

If you've been looking for thrilling tales of
contemporary passion and sensuous love stories
with taut, edge-of-the-seat suspense—
then you'll *love* Harlequin Intrigue!

Every month, you'll meet four new heroes
who are guaranteed to make your spine tingle
and your pulse pound. With them you'll enter
into the exciting world of Harlequin Intrigue—
where your life is on the line
and so is your heart!

THAT'S INTRIGUE—DYNAMIC
ROMANCE AT ITS BEST!

HARLEQUIN®

I N T R I G U E®

INT-GENR

LOOK FOR OUR FOUR FABULOUS MEN!

Each month some of today's bestselling authors bring
four new fabulous men to Harlequin American Romance.
Whether they're rebel ranchers, millionaire power brokers
or sexy single dads, they're all gallant princes—and
they're all ready to sweep you into lighthearted fantasies
and contemporary fairy tales where anything is possible
and where all your dreams come true!

You don't even have to make a wish…
Harlequin American Romance will grant your every desire!

Look for Harlequin American Romance
wherever Harlequin books are sold!

HAR-GEN

HARLEQUIN SUPERROMANCE®

...there's more to the story!

Superromance. A *big* satisfying read about unforget-
table characters. Each month we offer
four very different stories that range from family
drama to adventure and mystery, from highly emo-
tional stories to romantic comedies—and
much more! Stories about people you'll
believe in and care about. Stories too
compelling to put down....

Our authors are among today's *best* romance writ-
ers. You'll find familiar names and
talented newcomers. Many of them are
award winners—and you'll see why!

If you want the biggest and best
in romance fiction, you'll get it
from Superromance!

Available wherever Harlequin books are sold.

Look us up on-line at: http://www.romance.net

HS-GEN